"Keep an eye on those two outside,"

Longarm had told her, "and don't let me sleep too long..."

Kristen was leaning close over him.

"Longarm!" she whispered, her voice betraying her fear. "They're not down there in the alley. They're gone!"

Awake instantly, Longarm swung off the bed and reached for his Colt under the pillow. As he pulled it out, Kristen darted to a far corner. At that moment the door was flung open and the two men from the alley burst in.

Longarm slammed to the floor as both men cut loose with their sixguns. The powerful detonations caused the room's walls to reverberate powerfully. Hot lead slammed into the bed, sending a storm of feathers into the air...

TABOR EVANS

LONGARM

IN THE RUBY RANGE COUNTRY

A JOVE BOOK

LONGARM IN THE RUBY RANGE COUNTRY

A Jove Book/published by arrangement with
the author

PRINTING HISTORY
Jove edition/June 1986

ISBN: 0-515-08580-4

LONGARM
IN THE
RUBY RANGE COUNTRY

Chapter 1

Longarm had never seen it to fail. As soon as he took a vacation without his badge and tried to relax some, he ended up in a scrape worse than any Bill Vail could have engineered for him. Maybe it was something in his eyes, he reflected wearily, that hunted look a man gets when all he wants is to be left alone.

Seeking only a cool beer to rinse the alkali off his tonsils, Longarm had just entered the only saloon in Ruby, a sun-bleached town in a semi-arid valley near the Ruby Range. It was early in the afternoon, and he had long since made a rule never to undertake serious drinking until the sun went down and he was close enough to his hotel room to find it again without getting lost.

But as soon as he had shouldered up to the bar a few minutes before and ordered a beer, a hulking, heavy-set man with sullen eyes and a nose that had been broken several times moved up to the bar himself and shoved Longarm aside to give himself more room. Frowning in some irritation, Longarm moved down a bit, glancing at the big fellow as he did so. Though the man's attire was that of a working ranch hand, his broadcloth shirt and leather vest seemed a mite more expensive than what the usual working cowpoke wore. His Levi's were shoved down into the tops of his boots, and his .45 swung low on his right hip. His powerful shoulders continued to brush against Longarm's as the big man pounded on the bar with a huge, meaty fist.

"Another bottle, Ryan. Damn it! Bring me another god-damned bottle!"

Taking note of Longarm's presence for the first time, the big fellow snarled, "Give me room, damn you!" and struck aside Longarm's stein of beer, sending the glass skidding along the bar. "And get that shit from under my nose! If you're not man enough to drink whiskey, stay outa my way!"

Reaching out quickly, Longarm retrieved his now half-empty glass of beer. Again the big man pounded on the bar, shouting to the bartender for whiskey. A couple of patrons along the bar who had seen what happened to Longarm were laughing now, commenting to each other.

Longarm picked his glass up and threw its contents into the big fellow's face. The man stumbled back from the bar, pawing at his eyes. Others spun about to look. A couple of men laughed, others chuckled, and there was a steady shuffle of feet as the bar's patrons moved hastily out of the line of fire. The noise diminished rapidly, and those near the batwings stood on tiptoe and craned their necks to get a better view. Hurried, whispered murmurs ran through the place. Longarm detected a note of excitement, as if these patrons had been waiting all afternoon for this show—or one like it—to begin.

"Why, you dirty son of a bitch!" the big man cried furiously.

Putting down his empty stein, Longarm turned slowly. The big fellow's beefy face had gone purple with rage and he was still pawing at his eyes to clear out the beer. When he did clear them, he got a better look at Longarm and took a careful step back, suddenly wary.

"You fixin' to get your ass blowed off, mister?"

Drawing a sidearm and aiming in such cramped quarters was nearly impossible, Longarm figured. Besides, gunplay this close was always dicey. A dying man could still kill, his reflexes alone enough to blast a man into hell.

Longarm drew in a deep breath and forced himself to

2

smile. "Hell, no, stranger," he said mildly. "I'm not looking for trouble. I just came in here for a drink. If you want to forget it, I'll just order myself another beer and you can get your bottle and go on back to your table."

The big fellow's face relaxed. He straightened up, a ghost of a smile on his heavy face. "Suits me."

The tension broke. The barkeep placed the big man's bottle of whiskey on the bar. The big fellow reached out, took it, then pushed away from the bar. Men cleared their throats and conversation picked up again. One of the barkeeps farther down took up a handful of glasses and dunked them in a barrel of water; as he did so, they tinkled faintly. Longarm turned back to the bar to order his second beer.

Out of the corner of his eyes he saw the big fellow spin swiftly back around, his hand dropping to his sixgun. Wheeling smoothly away from the bar, Longarm was already drawing his Colt from his cross-draw rig. Before the big man's sixgun had cleared leather, Longarm's double-action .44 was kicking in his hand, filling the saloon with solid, reverberating sounds.

Longarm's Colt thundered three times in rapid succession. The first slug struck the man in the midriff, causing him to buckle forward and drop his sixgun. The second caught him high in the chest, causing him to reel back against a table. The third round smashed in the bridge of his nose, turning it into a gaping, bloody hole. The dead man slid to the floor. As he came to rest face up in the sawdust, a table slid over onto him. It made a kind of crude headstone for the damn fool.

There was a moment of awed silence as the repeated detonations rang between the walls. Then the thick clouds of gunsmoke cleared away. Longarm opened his Colt's loading gate and turned the cylinder, ejecting the spent casings. Lifting rounds from his side pocket, he reloaded. Careful to leave his hammer resting on an empty cylinder, he dropped the Colt back into his cross-draw rig and looked about him.

Two townsmen were hauling away the dead man, while

the swamper mopped up the mess, spreading fresh sawdust over the floor from a bucket he was carrying. From outside, Longarm could hear the storm of boots thumping along the plank sidewalks as men rushed from the saloon to spread the word. Others were bursting in to see and hear what had happened. Meanwhile, gathering about Longarm was a circle of gaping men, watching him in a mixture of awe and fear.

They had never seen a worm turn that fast before, Longarm reckoned.

Ignoring the crowd, Longarm turned back to the bar and made a second attempt to order his glass of beer. The response was immediate. He was served with a flourish. When he tried to pay, the barkeep pushed the coin back at him.

"From now on, mister," he informed Longarm with a broad wink, "your money's no good in here."

From all sides came pleased murmurs. Everyone, it seemed, was happy to be rid of that hulking brute Longarm had just despatched. Nodding his thanks to the barkeep, Longarm drank his fill. As he was putting down the stein, a hand rested lightly but firmly on his shoulder.

Longarm turned to see a hollow-cheeked fellow smiling at him. He wore his wide-brimmed hat at a cocky slant, the tips of his longish blond hair were bleached almost white from the sun, and his light blue eyes held a kind of feverish glow. He was almost as tall as Longarm and his shoulders were uncommonly square, but the most striking thing about him was the way his clothes hung on his sticklike frame. Unless the fellow tied himself down, Longarm was sure, a strong wind would blow him clean to Texas.

"I don't mean this to be a threat, mister," the fellow said, "but maybe you better finish that beer and get out of town pronto."

"That so?"

The man nodded unhappily. "It's not that I don't appreciate what you just did. You just stomped on big old Ham Walsh, like everyone in this town's been wanting to do for years. But now you'll have to answer to Dalton Cross."

"Who the hell's Dalton Cross?"

"The owner of the Cross D, the outfit Ham worked for."

Longarm nodded. He understood perfectly. Now that Longarm had killed Ham Walsh, he was going to have to answer to the man's boss. He already had a dim, unhappy idea where all this was going to lead.

"Let him come," Longarm said wearily. "If he's a reasonable man, he'll understand."

The gaunt fellow raised his eyebrows. "Do you think a reasonable man would hire an asshole like that?"

"You got a point."

"Right now, Dalton Cross is stocking up at Watson's General Store just down the street a ways. Soon's he hears about this, he'll be up here with the rest of his hired guns."

"I appreciate the warning. But I came in here to wash my tonsils, and I'm not running now. Join me in a beer, why don't you, and tell me more about this Dalton Cross."

The fellow grinned suddenly. "Sure," he said. "Why not?"

Longarm ordered two more beers and then led the way to a rear table. Every eye in the place followed them. Quite a few, Longarm was willing to bet, were hanging around for Cross's arrival.

Once they were seated, the stranger introduced himself as Harry Wilcox.

"Name's Custis Long," Longarm replied. "My friends call me Longarm." He leaned back in his chair and sipped his beer. "The fact is, I came west from Denver to see an old friend who needs some help. I had no intention to rile anybody, least of all this fellow Walsh or his boss."

"This friend of yours live in town, does he?"

"It ain't a he. It's a she."

"Then you have come to rescue a lady in distress." Harry sipped his beer and nodded agreeably. "Now I understand perfectly."

"No, you don't. She's married—happily married, as a matter of fact."

"Now I *am* confused."

5

"I said 'friend' before, and I meant that."

"What seems to be her problem?"

"She's ranching somewhere up in the Rubies and is having some trouble with her neighbors."

Harry put down his glass of beer and looked shrewdly at Longarm. "Could this friend of yours possibly own a ranch next to the Cross D?"

"She did mention that brand."

"Then your friend owns the Lazy S spread. Right?"

Longarm smiled. "That's her and Bill's brand, all right."

"Thought so. No wonder she'd be callin' for help. The Lazy S is the only ranch standin' up to the Cross D." Harry leaned back in his chair and smiled ironically at Longarm. "Well, sir, I'd say you are one fast worker."

"What do you mean?"

"Ham Walsh was the Cross D's foreman. He's the one been causin' trouble for the Lazy S and the Basque sheepherders up there. Ham Walsh was Cross's point man, someone he could count on to break heads and take the brunt of the resentment and bloodletting Cross himself was causin'."

Longarm leaned back and considered his situation. He had received the letter from Sally Adams a couple of weeks back. She had mentioned how much she loved the ranch and how hard she and her husband Bill had been working to make it prosper. Then she'd gone on to ask why he hadn't accepted her many invitations to take a vacation from the mile-high city and stay with her and Bill for a few weeks. Only in passing had she indicated that they were having some difficulty, mentioning in particular the adjacent Cross D spread.

But Longarm had had no difficulty reading between the lines. The letter had been a plea for help. After giving it some thought, Longarm had gone to Marshal Vail to ask for some time off. Vail given him no argument. Of late, as Vail well knew, Longarm had been carrying a pretty heavy load in Denver town, and the marshal knew just how much his best deputy wanted to shake the mile-high city. And now, just a few hours from the Ruby Range country, Longarm was getting a pretty clear picture of the kind of trouble Sally and Bill were up against.

"You know where the Lazy S is?" Longarm asked Harry.

"Sure."

"Then how about you and me riding out there?"

Harry considered the idea quickly, then nodded. "Sure. Why not? I've been wanting to shake the dust of this town."

"Good. My gear's in the livery stable. By the way, are you armed?"

Harry patted a slight bulge on the left side of his coat. "Like you," he said, "I keep my weapon out of sight. It's in my belt."

"What do you shoot?"

"A Starr Army .44. Double-action."

Longarm consulted his watch. It was a little before three. He looked up at Harry as he replaced the watch in his vest pocket. "How long a ride is it to the Lazy S?"

"Four, maybe five hours, I'd say."

Longarm nodded.

Harry suddenly grinned as his eye followed the gold-washed chain that led from Longarm's watch to the bulge of the twin-barrel .44-calibre derringer resting in his fob pocket. "Don't I see a cheater in that fob pocket?" he asked.

Longarm smiled. "You have good eyes."

"Derringer?"

"It makes a nice surprise, at times."

"Why didn't you use it on Ham?"

"I knew I could outdraw him. All I needed was enough room. Besides, I don't like to advertise the derringer."

"Makes sense."

"Finish your drink and we'll be on our way."

Harry tipped the stein up and downed the beer. Some of it must have gone down the wrong way. Slamming the empty stein down onto the table, he bent his head over and began coughing violently, so violently that Longarm got to his feet to pound his back. But Harry shook his head and pushed

7

Longarm away, then held a handkerchief to his mouth as the violent siege of coughing slowly subsided.

Through it all, Longarm noted that few of the saloon's patrons paid much attention to Harry's coughing spell. This violent coughing spasm was evidently something that happened quite frequently to Harry. Longarm suddenly understood why Harry was so thin, his face so pale, and why his eyes burned with such a bright, hectic gleam. Wilcox was a consumptive, and had drifted out here to the high country, like so many others, in hopes of escaping the ravages of his disease.

Dabbing his mouth and smiling apologetically at Longarm, Harry sat up. "You must forgive me. That's the first bad spell I've had in days."

"Forget it. You ready now?"

Harry nodded and got to his feet.

They pushed through the crowded saloon and were striding out onto the porch when six riders pulled their horses to a dusty halt in front of the saloon. As his men watched, the leader dismounted and strode up onto the porch.

Longarm knew at once that this was the owner of the Cross D. Dalton Cross was a tall, powerfully built man in his late forties. He had a thick, tobacco-stained mustache drooping over his mouth, a granite jaw, and eyes that peered with fierce combativeness out from under a broad, powerful brow.

"You the one shot my ramrod?" Cross asked Longarm, taking a stance in front of him, his feet apart, braced for trouble.

"I reckon so," Longarm replied easily.

"What'd he do?"

"He had bad manners. Very bad."

Cross looked shrewdly at Longarm. "Ham was always a fool when he got liquored up. But he was a Cross D rider and my foreman."

"Pick a better man next time."

"What in hell's your name, stranger?"

"Rutherford B. Hayes," Longarm replied shortly, "and I'll thank you to get out of my way."

From behind Longarm, the saloon's patrons, crowding up to the batwings and the windows, burst into smothered laughter. Cross was not amused, however. His face went tight with anger. His men, still sitting their mounts, leaned forward, their faces taut, like hounds straining on their leashes.

"Damn it!" Cross demanded. "Tell me who you are, or I'll wring it out of you!"

Longarm just laughed at the man and strode on past him, brushing him roughly aside. Infuriated, Cross took a step back, digging clumsily for his gun. Swinging back around, Longarm drew his .44 easily and lifted the bore so the big cattleman could peer down its bore.

Cross dropped his sixgun back into his holster. His men, however, were not that well disciplined, and went for their irons. One rider, a mite too anxious, began blasting at Longarm. A bullet chewed a hole in the porch floor at Longarm's feet. Another one shattered the saloon window. What saved Longarm was the man's horse. It was rearing frantically, throwing off the rider's aim. Before Longarm could turn on him, Harry's sixgun roared, and the Cross D rider dropped his gun and slipped crookedly off his horse, a bullet in his shoulder.

Swinging around to cover the rest of the riders, Longarm and Harry moved back slowly, keeping Cross and his riders in their line of sight. Behind him, Longarm could hear the saloon's patrons stampeding back from the windows. He didn't blame them. It looked as if all hell was about to break loose. But Cross straightened up and turned angrily on his riders.

"Next man starts throwin' lead, I'll send a bullet up his ass! This here's my fight! Burt! Sledge! Take that damn fool over to the barbershop and get him fixed up. I don't care how bad he's hurt, he'll be ridin' back with us tonight, and that should teach him plenty."

9

Longarm and Harry holstered their guns, descended the porch steps, and walked across the street to the livery.

A few moments later, as the two men rode out of the livery and headed out of town, Dalton Cross, watching from the saloon doorway, called one of his riders to him. The fellow dismounted quickly and pounded up onto the porch.

"Go on back down to Watson's and get what supplies you need," Cross told the rider. "I want you to go after Ham's brother. Tell him there's a thousand dollars in it for him if he comes back here with you and another thousand when he finishes off the man who killed his brother."

"But, Mr. Cross," the rider said nervously, "I don't know where Ham's brother is!"

"I'm gonna tell you, damn it! Just shut up and listen. Pete's in Ely City, running a faro game in the Gold Nugget. You won't have no trouble finding him. Just tell him what happened to Ham. That'll bring him . . . that and the money."

"Supposin' it don't?"

"God damn it, Jeeter! Don't argue with me. Just ride out now and do what I said!"

Hurrying off the porch, Jeeter mounted up and hauled his horse brutally around. In a moment he had lifted his mount to a lope as he rode swiftly back down the street.

Cross beckoned to another rider still astride his horse at the hitch rack. He was a slovenly, pocked man with a gray face and mean, button-like eyes. "Follow that tall bastard who killed Ham," Cross told the man. "I want to know where he's goin' and what he's doin' in this country."

The pocked rider pulled his horse back from the hitch rack and rode out of town.

Watching him ride off, Cross felt the bottled, stomach-churning fury inside him abate somewhat. He had done enough for now. That tall son of a bitch would pay for this afternoon's insolence. He would see to that. For now, it was just a matter of biding his time. Hell, it even gave him something to look forward to.

He left his remaining riders to sit their horses in the hot sun and pushed through the Ruby's batwings. A drink was what he needed, something to calm his down. But as he approached the bar, every man in the place suddenly shut his mouth and looked away from him. He'd find no sociability here, no friendly voice to ease his embarrassment.

One of those men who had run down to the general store to tell him of Ham's death had also told Cross that the barkeep Ryan had been so pleased he had told the tall son of a bitch that his drinks were on the house. And the patrons in the place had cheered. Recalling this now, Cross forced himself to say nothing to Ryan as he pulled his bottle toward him and poured his drink.

He was willing to wait. There would come a time when he would be the biggest cattleman in the Rubies. Then he'd strip the hide off every man in this room, starting with the barkeep.

Chapter 2

"I didn't see much sign of the law in Ruby," Longarm commented to Harry as the two of them, riding side by side, lifted higher into the Ruby Range.

"There ain't any, Longarm. Except what the Cross D sets down."

"What about the Mormons hereabouts?"

"The Mormons who've settled in these hills are pretty damn close to outlaws, too, Longarm, with bands of Destroying Angels imposing their own brand of Mormonism. Seems like it's a bit hard for them Saints to stick to just one woman, once they've found out how much fun a variety can be."

"Can't see how they do it," Longarm commented, a sly grin lighting his lean features. "I have trouble handling 'em one at a time."

"They got settlements all over in these mountains," Harry went on, "and none of them eager to advertise their presence."

"Dangerous, are they?"

Harry chuckled. "As like as not they welcome most strangers with a load of buckshot."

"Don't see what they're so worried about," Longarm mused. "From what I've seen of their women, they can have them—a dozen at a time, if that's their pleasure. I figure it's a service to humanity to give creatures as grim-looking as them Mormon females a home and a chance to breed."

13

Harry laughed. "Reckon so."

Without glancing at the trail behind them, Longarm remarked, "We got a friend tailing us. He's been there since we left Ruby."

"I see him too. Wondered if you did. He's one of Cross's riders."

"What's he called?"

"Sam Connell."

"Maybe we ought to give Sam a surprise. I don't want him to catch on to where we're heading."

"What've you got in mind?"

"First chance we get, take my horse and ride on without me for a mile or so, then circle back."

Harry nodded without a word.

As they rose higher into the Ruby Range, Longarm was relieved to put behind him the arid land he had ridden across to get here. The ride down here to the Ruby Range had been more than a little depressing. A Western Pacific train had taken him to Wells, Nevada, and from there it had been a grueling two days' ride to Ruby Lake and that interesting glass of beer in the town of Ruby.

Longarm had already had occasion to traverse the salt flats between the Rubies and Salt Lake City, and he never wanted that pleasure again. This high, barren basin did not attract him, and neither did this Ruby Range. It was a bleak, treacherous land; as he rode over it, he wondered at the desperation that sent men and their women into such places to wrest a living and made cattlemen like Dalton Cross willing to kill for it.

The higher peaks and ridges of the Rubies were like islands in the bleak basin land, cooler and wetter islands that offered a blessed relief from the grim stretches of salt flats below. Occasionally, Longarm was able to see back down the slope at Ruby Lake, fed by natural drainage from the range. But as for the range itself, there was nothing red or ruby-colored within sight. The Ruby Range got its name from early greenhorns who thought the garnets showing here

14

and there in the mostly granitic and volcanic rock were gems of pure ruby and other precious stones. Before the sad truth could be broadcast, it was too late. The prospectors had already swarmed in, and Ruby Range it had become.

Longarm and Harry began riding past stands of piñon pine and juniper, and before long a carpet of grass began to take hold. They were reaching a cooler, more hospitable altitude. Mule deer and desert bighorn occasionally broke from cover.

"This Adams woman," Harry said, pulling his horse back some so the two men could converse more easily, "the one you're comin' to help. She an old flame, is she?"

Ordinarily Longarm did not answer such personal questions or even suffer them to be asked. But he liked Harry Wilcox and he replied without pause that he had met Sally in Denver. She had wanted to marry him, he went on, but he had declined. As he had explained it to her, a man in his line of work did not lightly take on the responsibilities of marriage, and besides, he did not think himself near ready for such an undertaking. Then he had introduced the girl to the man who was now her husband, Bill Adams. Bill had had his share of trouble with the law and the bottle, but he had managed to pull himself together, and as luck would have it, Sally and Bill hit it off from the first. After their marriage they had come out here to take over a ranch Sally's father left her. The ranch boasted well-watered range deep in the Rubies. Now, after less than two years, Sally had written him a letter calling for help—and, having just met Dalton Cross, Longarm understood why.

"You'll need an army to stop Cross," Harry told Longarm.

"Maybe yes, maybe no," Longarm replied. "Let's see how the land lies before we start calling for help."

Ahead of them on the trail, rearing up from behind a clump of pine, Longarm caught sight of a towering shoulder of rock, broad at the base and sloping gradually to a cap at the top.

"As soon as we get beyond that rock," Longarm told Harry, "I'll dismount. Take my horse's lead then and do what I said before. Just give me enough time before doubling back."

Harry nodded.

As soon as the rock shielded them from the trail behind, Longarm dismounted and snaked his Winchester from his saddle scabbard. Then he tossed the reins to Harry. As Harry disappeared up the trail, Longarm pulled himself up the sloping side of the rock like a big cat, moving from toehold to toehold until he found a perch on a ledge above the trail. Jacking a fresh round into his Winchester, he settled down to wait.

Not long after, the rider Harry had identified as Sam Connell appeared on the trail below him, riding slumped over his saddle horn. His unshaven face was sallow and scarred with old pockmarks. His eyes, peering out from under his hatbrim, shifted furtively as he rode. He was a Cross D gunslick, all right. Longarm had seen him among Cross's riders pulled up in front of the saloon.

Longarm waited until the rider was almost directly under him before he spoke. "Hold it right there, mister."

The rider pulled up quickly, his hand dropping automatically to his sixgun.

"I wouldn't if I were you," Longarm told him.

The man glanced up, shoving his hatbrim off his forehead to get a better view of Longarm. When he saw Longarm's grinning face behind the rifle's muzzle, he slumped angrily in his saddle and slowly raised both hands over his head.

"Ain't no law against usin' this trail, is there?" he demanded.

"Hell, no. I been using it right along."

"So why you throwin' down on me?"

"I'm just an ornery son of a bitch, looks like. Unbuckle your gunbelt and let it fall to the ground. Then toss your rifle down alongside it. Do it real slow."

"You son of a bitch," the rider muttered as he unbuckled

16

his gunbelt. "Wait'll Cross hears about this."

"You mean *he's* the one owns this trail?"

The rider leaned carefully forward and lifted his Winchester from its scabbard, then dropped it carefully to the ground beside the gunbelt. "He owns just about everything in these hills worth owning," the man replied. "An' anything he don't own, he trashes. You'll find that out soon enough."

"You want to explain that remark, mister?"

"Sure," the fellow replied, mean pleasure lighting his face. "From the look of it, you're headin' for the Lazy S. If you are, you ain't gonna find much left."

Longarm was reluctant to show concern. It would give this rider just the information he wanted. "I don't know what you're talking about, Sam," Longarm said, "but if it makes you happy to think that's where I'm heading, why, you go right ahead."

"You sure as hell don't act like no Mormon," said Connell.

"How's a Mormon supposed to act?"

"Hell, I can't answer that," the man replied evasively.

"Sam, you ever hear of the Destroying Angels?"

"Sure."

"You think maybe *that's* the way a Mormon's supposed to act."

Sam frowned up at Longarm. "Jesus! You one of them?"

Longarm smiled. "I didn't say I was. I just asked you a question."

"Yeah," the rider said. "Sure."

Longarm nodded shrewdly, as if that settled the matter. "All right, then," he said. "Don't get any funny ideas, Sam. Just stay where you are."

Longarm ducked back off the ledge and picked his way swiftly down the steep rockface. When he reached the trail, he told the sullen rider to dismount.

"What're you goin' to do?" Sam asked, dismounting. "I ain't got no quarrel with you Mormons. I was just ridin' along this here trail."

"Well, that's good to know. Take off your boots."

17

For a moment the Cross D rider looked with some puzzlement at Longarm. Then, with a weary, defeated shrug, he sat back on a boulder and pulled off both boots. Since Sam wore no stockings under the boots, the assault on Longarm's nose was almost lethal. Longarm kicked the boots off the trail. As they disappeared into a gully below the trail, Sam groaned.

Next, Longarm emptied the man's six-shooter and rifle and kicked the cartridges off the trail, flinging the gunbelt after them. Then Longarm grabbed the reins to Sam's mount, swung up into the saddle, and looked down at the unhappy man standing barefoot in the trail.

"Well, Sam, I'm sorry to leave you afoot; but you know the Saints don't like Gentiles messing in church business."

"It wasn't my idea. Cross told me to follow you two."

Longarm smiled. "Well, then. This should put you in real solid with your boss—especially when he sees you walking barefoot. If you still can, that is. Tell him I'll send this horse back when I'm through with it."

Sam said nothing. He didn't have to. His eyes said all that was necessary. From this moment on, Longarm knew, he had created in Sam Connell an enemy who would not rest until he had made Longarm pay for this humiliation.

With a curt nod, Longarm wheeled Connell's mount and rode on down the trail.

Fuming, Sam watched him ride off. If it were the last thing he ever did, he would get that son of a bitch someday; but right now he had other things to worry about. Dalton Cross, for one thing. That bastard of a Destroying Angel would probably release his horse farther down the trail, and the dumb brute would gallop into the Cross D a hell of a lot sooner than Sam would.

That would make him a laughingstock. He could see Cross's face now, dark with contempt, his mouth twisting with sarcasm. Once more Sam had failed to live up to his boss's expectations.

Sam Connell was sick of it. He no longer wanted to ride for the Cross D. Hell, after this, he wouldn't be able to. Cross might just run him off without even giving him his back pay.

The hell with Cross! He'd go on to Little Eden, maybe warn that crazy Elder Booth about this here Destroying Angel in the neighborhood. Sure. That was it. Maybe he could find some kind of a job in Little Eden. And even if he didn't, anything was better than walking all the way back to the Cross D—and then have to deal with all the grinning faces.

Slowly, carefully, cursing bitterly all the while, Sam clambered on bare foot down the steep slope, determined to find his boots, at least.

A few minutes later, Longarm met Harry circling back with his own horse. Dismounting, he slapped the Cross D rider's mount on the flank and sent him off into a shaded ravine, confident that the animal would eventually find his way back to the Cross D. Mounting up, he told Harry he was pretty sure he had convinced the Cross D rider he was a Mormon, a member of the Destroying Angels. Harry laughed.

Then Longarm mentioned what the rider had said about the Lazy S.

Harry frowned in sudden concern. "Now that reminds me," he said. "When Cross's boys were in the general store, there was some loose talk goin' around about trashing a ranch up here somewhere."

Longarm nodded grimly. "I don't like the sound of it."

There was no more conversation after that as the two men lifted their mounts to a steady lope. When they pulled up on a hogback a few hours before sundown to look across a swale at what remained of the Lazy S, the smell of burning still hung in the air. The ranch house and the bunkhouse remained standing, but the two barns were a smoking ruin.

"That son of a bitch," Longarm said tightly, as he put his mount on down the slope. He and Harry were almost to the compound when a woman Longarm recognized stepped out of the ranch house, a shotgun in her hand.

"Don't shoot, Sally!" Longarm called to her. "It's me!"

"Custis!"

Dropping the shotgun, she raced toward him. He dismounted and waited for her with open arms. She plunged into his embrace, wrapping her arms about him. Then, still holding onto him as tightly as she could, she began to sob.

He held her until the storm subsided, then pushed her gently away and looked down into her small face. She had real dark hair she cut short, a pug nose, and freckles still, with blue eyes as luminous as the sky, only now they were clouded up some and ready to let go again any minute.

"At least you saved the house," he told her. "The barns can be built up again soon enough."

"It ain't just that, Longarm."

"What else, then?"

She blinked away her tears and with a quick movement brushed the hair off her forehead. "Later," she told him. "I can't tell you out here." She turned her gaze for the first time on Harry Wilcox.

"This here's my friend, Harry," Longarm told her. "He's come along to help. He's already been considerable help. Harry, meet Sally Adams."

Harry tipped his hat to Sally and she nodded back, frowning. "Maybe I seen you before, Harry. In Ruby?"

"The saloon, more than likely," Harry suggested gently.

"Yes," she agreed. "When I was looking for my husband."

"Bill's fallen off the wagon?" Longarm asked, immediately concerned.

"So many times, I lost count," Sally replied with weary exasperation. "Come inside. We'll talk there. Oh, Custis, I'm so glad you came!"

Longarm chuckled and tucked her hand into the crook of his arm as he and Harry escorted her back to the ranch house. They were almost there when a wiry old man emerged from the bunkhouse with a huge Walker Colt and a Sharps rifle. When he pulled up beside them, Sally introduced him as Abe, her hired man. Abe looked to be close to sixty and walked with the painful, bowed legs of an ex-puncher. His face was as wrinkled as old leather and looked just as worn. But he gave both Longarm and Harry a firm handshake, and his eyes were still alert.

As Abe led their horses away, Longarm and Harry continued into the ranch house with Sally.

"Where's Bill?" Longarm asked, slumping gratefully down at the kitchen table.

Sally reached down the Arbuckle and the coffee pot. "He's gone after Dalton Cross."

"He's what?"

"That's what he said. As soon as we drove off them Cross D apes, Bill told me to hold the fort with Abe while he went after Cross. He'd been drinking, Custis. There was nothing I could do to stop him."

"You could have shot him."

She smiled wanly. "I thought of that, believe me. Custis, I'm at the end of my rope with Bill. He's a wonderful, sweet man, and the hardest worker you ever saw—when he's sober."

"How often is that?"

"Hardly ever, Longarm, lately."

"Maybe it's this awful heat."

"I don't know what it is, and I no longer care."

"All right, Sally. All right. Now, when did this attack by Cross's men happen?"

"Last night."

"Did you get any of them?"

"I think we wounded a couple. It was Abe who opened up on them first. He caught them sneaking close to the barn. He and Bill drove them off, but not before they almost burned us out. We were lucky to keep it to the barns. But, Longarm, we lost so much grain and fodder for the horses!"

"Did you save the stock?"

21

"Yes. But that ain't all of it, Custis."

She turned her back on the coffee pot and folded her arms, her face grim. "Cross says we got to clear out or the next time he'll finish what he started last night."

"He's serious about driving you out, all right," said Longarm.

"He wants this land," Sally said.

"Why is it so special?"

Sally smiled. "We got the only good year-round source of water within twenty miles. We've been sharing it with a Mormon settlement. They've been using it to irrigate their crops."

"They ain't going to like what Cross is doing then."

"I've spoken to their elder. He thinks he can deal with Cross. What he doesn't know is that Cross is as anxious to drive them off as he is to drive Bill and me off."

"He's greedy."

"It's more than that, Custis. He's a sick man. Land is his opiate. He already has enough—more than enough—for his spread."

"Where's he from?"

Sally turned back to the coffee. "Texas. He was run out of there by nesters. They ruined the land, then abandoned it. I've heard the story a hundred times. This time he's going to be the one to run others off."

Longarm nodded. Sally brought him and Harry their coffee, then placed a jar full of doughnuts down in front of them. "This'll hold you until I can fix you a proper meal," she told them.

"Thanks, Sally."

Pausing beside him, she rested a hand on his shoulder and gazed fondly into his eyes. "I can't believe you're here, Custis. You've no idea how much better I feel."

"I'm worried about Bill."

"I'm not," she snapped, pulling back, her eyes cold. "I stopped worryin' about him a long time ago."

"Going up against Cross alone might kill him."

She laughed coldly. "You know what? Now that I think of it, that was maybe just liquor talking. I've heard him blusterin' and boastin' of what he'd do if Cross gave him any more trouble. It never came to anything. The way I see it, he probably rode into Ruby first to tank up, and never got any farther."

"We didn't pass him on the way here. And when we were in Ruby we didn't see any sign of him. If he was in that saloon, I sure as hell wouldn't have missed him."

Sally was grimly determined to see things her way. She shook her head firmly. "You just missed him, that's all. Maybe he's sleepin' it off in some shady spot off the trail somewhere."

"You say he left here angry."

"Angry as a wet hornet, and with a bottle in his back pocket. Don't you see, Custis? This is just one more excuse for him to drink."

"You're sure of that?"

"I'm his wife," she said bitterly.

Longarm studied Sally for a moment, aware suddenly how cold a woman could get once she had turned on a man. Once that happened, nothing good in the past counted for a thing. There was no stone on earth harder than the woman's heart.

Sally returned to the stove to fix their meal. As she worked, Longarm and Harry went outside to look around. Abe joined them as they inspected the damage. It was considerable. Both barns would have to be rebuilt from the ground up. Only luck had kept the blacksmith shop from going up also. A small portion of the bunkhouse roof was singed. The big corral in back of where the horse barn had been was thick with horseflesh, however, and farther down the slope, Longarm could see a sizable herd. Lazy S sheep, looking like tiny bits of gray fluff, were ranging high into the rocky hills above them.

The three of them returned finally to the barn's smouldering ruin. Plucking a grass stem and chewing on it thought-

23

fully, Abe said, "I figure if we didn't catch them when we did, they would've finished us off good and proper. This time we was lucky."

"There won't be a next time, Abe," Longarm told the man.

At that moment Sally stepped out onto the low porch and called them to their meal. Bidding Abe good night, Longarm returned with Harry to the ranch house for their promised supper. Sally had not stinted. It was a fine meal, with dumplings and both beef and mutton heaped high on platters. The homemade bread was sliced thick and still warm from the oven. It was a meal worth riding a long way for, and both men told her close to the same thing.

"You two must be tired," she told them as she cleared the table.

Longarm nodded. "I could use some shuteye. It was a long, dry ride from Wells. And when I got to Ruby, I wasn't exactly made to feel welcome."

"Then you'll sleep in here tonight," she told him. "I want a man around. I want to hear his heavy breathing in the darkness. Then maybe I'll feel safe."

Smiling, Harry said, "I'll sleep in the bunkhouse with Abe."

Sally shrugged. "You don't have to. I can make a bed up for you here in the kitchen."

"The bunkhouse is fine, Sally."

"You sure you wouldn't mind?"

"Not unless Abe snores."

Sally laughed. "I wish I knew."

"I'll give you a first-hand report in the morning," Harry told her, getting up from the table.

Thanking her again for the meal, he took his leave and left the ranch house. Sally showed Longarm the spare bedroom and turned down the bed for him. Longarm undressed, blew out the lantern, and rested back on the soft down, his head whirling, his thoughts on Bill. He hoped Sally was right—that Bill was tanked out somewhere, sleeping it off.

24

One man going against that crew was worse than foolhardy. It was suicide.

There was a light rap on his door. Turning his head to face the door, he said, "Come in, Sally."

Dressed only in her long nightgown, Sally entered, her eyes glowing—only it was not tears making them glow this time. He saw she had not bothered to button the long gown and as she walked closer, she allowed it to fall open. Her small, taut breasts, resembled pale lamps in the moonlit room, and the dark triangle of her pubis stood out sharply against the pale alabaster of her firm belly and thighs. He felt a near-painful tightening in his groin and realized that, despite his fatigue, from the moment her rap sounded on the door, he had begun to come to life down there.

"Are you surprised?" she asked him, pausing beside his bed to let her nightgown slip to the floor.

"I guess not, judging from the way you talked about Bill."

"You think I'm horrid, don't you?"

"Right now, I'd rather not think," he said, reaching up for her.

With a grateful rush, she fell upon him, the warmth of her body enclosing his with a suddenness that filled him with a fierce urgency. He swung his arm around her narrow waist and swept her to him. Both knees coming down on each side of her, he reached his big hand under her buttocks and pulled her up at the same time he plunged down into her. The tip of his erection plowed recklessly past her pubis and plunged deep into her.

"Ah...!" she cried, in ecstasy. "Oh, Custis...!"

Her arms clasped about his neck, she swung her legs up eagerly, crossing her ankles behind his back. Groaning with desire, she swung up under him, pulling his enormous erection still deeper into her.

From the first, their coupling was like a grim battle that progressed with a wild, mindless urgency. Panting like animals, they had at each other, murmuring, biting, until

25

Longarm found himself slamming violently down into her, his need so brutal and overpowering that when he kissed her on the lips she had to pull away finally, gasping—and laughing.

Then he was beyond the point of no return, rushing headlong to his climax. Plunging over the crest, Sally tumbled over it with him, laughing and crying at the same time.

Then, with her head tucked next to his, she panted wildly in his ear, murmuring his name over and over, until at last she released him, allowing Longarm to roll over and look into her glowing, perspiring face.

"You act like it's been a long time," he told her.

"It has."

"How come?"

"Don't you know what happens to drunks when they drink too much?"

Longarm nodded unhappily. He knew what happened. Liquor could make a man want to, all right—but it could sure throw a monkey wrench into his ability to do so. And too much liquor could entirely destroy a man's potency. It surprised Longarm that more men did not know this. It was one of the reasons why Longarm had such respect for whores. They had this problem to deal with constantly, and on the whole they managed to handle it with compassion and, in some cases, success.

But it took a whore with a lot of imagination and patience. Where Bill was concerned, Sally had obviously lost it completely.

"More," she said.

He leaned back and grinned at her. "Go slow," he said. "Take it easy this time."

She giggled. "Poor man. You runnin' out of steam?"

She kissed him, hard, hungrily. Then her fingers took over the job of building him back up. The moment he was erect, she straddled him eagerly, slipping him deep inside her. Then, sucking in her breath luxuriantly, she leaned her head back and began to rock slowly, ever so slowly. Long-arm closed his eyes and let her have her way with him as he felt the fire begin to build a second time in his loins. He lost track of time, but when he heard her fierce, sharp cries, he opened his eyes, reached up for her hips, grabbed them with both hands, and began slamming her up and down upon him.

"Oh yes!" she cried. "Yes! Harder, deeper, Custis!"

He complied, slamming her down upon him with reck-lessness. He was no longer able to hold back, and before long, he was stretching as far as the horizon, his entire body aflame, as he sent spasm after spasm into her tight, quivering vagina.

With a high, keening cry, Sally collapsed forward onto his massive chest, her mouth half open, her eyes heavy.

As he felt himself come out of her, he let his heavy hand drop onto her small head. "How's that?" he whispered. "You satisfied?"

She kissed the mat of hair on his chest, then moved up so his lips could encircle her nipples. They were still hard, erect, thrusting—like nails.

"Until the next time," she told him, her laughter deep and seductive, as she reached down for him again.

After the next time, they lay for a long while in each other's arms without uttering a sound. At length, Sally stirred.

"I asked you before if you thought I was horrid, and you said you'd rather not think about it. Can you think about it now?"

"Sure."

"Do you?"

"I figure maybe that was a mistake we made back there in Denver. Bill was not for you, and I shouldn't have in-troduced you."

"You mean it's all your fault?"

"Something like that. Yes."

27

"You men. You have such fabulous egos. No, Custis. I am responsible for marrying Bill, not you. I fell in love with Bill, and that was my mistake, no one else's."

"Do you still love him?"

"I suppose I do, in a way—like a mother loves an errant child. But it isn't anything more than that. How can a woman love a man she can't respect? And I find it very difficult to respect a man who pees in his pants and shits on the floor, and then cries about it afterward, like a baby. I wanted children, Custis, but I'd be worse than a fool to have any with this man."

"So you've been staying away from him."

"It hasn't been all that hard to do, Custis."

"For you, maybe. But what about him?"

"I told you the problem he has. Besides, I honestly don't think he notices. Face it, Custis, he's a drunkard. It's as simple—and as terrible—as that."

Longarm said nothing more, and Sally lapsed into silence. After a while, she got up from the bed, slipped her nightgown back on, then leaned her face close to his and kissed him warmly and gently on his lips.

"Good night, Custis. Thanks for coming. I really needed you."

He smiled up at her. She turned and glided silently across the room and let herself out. He heard the door close softly behind her, then shut his eyes and almost immediately drifted off, his last thoughts not of Sally, but of Bill.

The drunkard, as she called him . . .

Chapter 3

Longarm came awake suddenly and glanced out the window.
Dawn had lightened the sky over the hills, but the yard itself
was still pitch dark. What had awakened him was the steady,
growing thunder of horses' hooves. He jumped out of bed
and pulled his Colt from his holster, then ducked down
beside the window. It sounded like Cross's riders come to
finish the job they had started the night before.

Sally burst into his room and crouched beside him. "Is
it Cross?" she asked. "Has he come again?"

"Can't see for sure, damn it! Not enough light."

A storm of horsemen materialized out of the pre-dawn
darkness. As they clattered past the front of the ranch house,
Longarm saw something large and misshapen flung from
one of the horses. It landed in front of the doorway. In a
moment the riders were whirling away again into the darkness, one or two sending shots into the sky out of sheer
exuberance.

Pulling on his pants, Longarm followed Sally to the door.
She opened it first, then screamed and dropped to the side
of the broken form that moved sluggishly on the ground
before her, moaning in pain.

Reaching Sally's side, Longarm looked down into the
purpled, barely recognizable face of Bill Adams as he gazed
pitiably up at his wife. The puffed slits that hid his eyes
flickered painfully. His swollen, mangled lips twisted in

pain, and the groans that continued to escape his throat seemed torn from the roots of his soul.

"Legs . . . my legs . . ." he whispered thickly.

Sally took Bill's head in her lap and bent over it, rocking.

By that time Harry and Abe had joined Longarm.

"We've got to get Bill inside," Longarm told Sally.

As gently as he could, Abe pulled Sally away from Bill. Longarm and Harry lifted the man as gently as they could, doing their best to keep Bill's legs straight. Bill groaned and thrashed feebly as they carried him inside, then followed Sally into the room Longarm had just left.

They tried to put Bill down without hurting him, but the moment his legs touched the bed, Bill uttered a scream so filled with agony that both men winced in sympathy. Longarm lit a lamp quickly and held it over Bill to examine his legs. Beside him, Harry gasped.

Bill's knees were purpled, bloody knobs, the bones and kneecaps shattered by repeated blows. From the knees down, both legs were bent grotesquely outward, the way no legs properly attached ever should. They looked like the legs of a discarded doll. All that still attached the legs to Bill's knees were shreds of torn cartilage and bloodied skin.

"Longarm!" Bill gasped suddenly, as recognition flooded his face. "My God! Is it you?"

"It's me, all right," Longarm told him, leaning close. "Sorry I didn't get here sooner, Bill."

"Well, you came! That's the good part."

"Who did this to you, Bill?"

"Cross's men. I was a fool! I rode right into the Cross D and demanded Cross come out. He didn't even bother to show himself. Then someone roped me from behind and pulled me from my horse. That was when Cross's men went to work on me . . . !"

He squeezed his eyes shut then and began to writhe in pain. He must have stirred inadvertently, causing what was left of his legs to move. Groaning softly, he began turning his head back and forth in a fierce, terrible agony.

30

"Try to lie still, Bill," Longarm told him, "till we fix you up."

His eyes still closed tightly, he muttered, "My legs, Longarm. My legs . . ."

At that moment Sally stepped forward, gasping as she saw more closely now what had been done to Bill's legs.

"Both legs are broken, looks like," Longarm whispered to her. "At the knees."

Sally moved closer to the moaning, twisting form on the bed and went down on her knees. Reaching out, she took Bill's hand in hers, tears streaming down her face.

Bill opened his eyes and turned his head to look at her. "Sally, give me something for this pain," he gasped. "Anything . . . please!"

Sally turned her head to glance up at Abe. "Get the whiskey," she told him.

Abe vanished from the room. Leaving Bill with Sally, Longarm and Harry followed Abe from the room and slumped down at the kitchen table. Each man kept his own counsel as Sally worked swiftly behind them, heating water and ripping cotton cloth into bandages. The yard outside the ranch house slowly lightened. It was full daylight when Sally joined them.

"Abe's with him now," she told them, slumping down in a chair across from them. "He's resting quietly now, but he's hurt fearfully." Sally was obviously distraught. "I've never seen such a cruel and terrible beating! How could Cross let his men do this? He must be an animal!"

"If Bill was out to kill Cross, and Cross caught him at it, I'd say Bill's lucky to be alive."

Sally shuddered. "And I thought he was just sleeping it off somewhere . . . that he would never have had the . . ." She couldn't finish.

"Sally," Longarm told her, "Bill might lose his life if he isn't seen to by a good doc—and soon. Is there anyone nearby?"

"In the Mormon settlement, Little Eden. He's a Gentile,

but the Mormons keep him well fed and give him plenty of valley tan so he won't run off."

"Valley tan?"

"Mormon moonshine," Sally replied tartly. "They ain't allowed to drink whiskey, so this is what they use instead. It does the job nicely, I understand."

"That it does," chuckled Harry.

"Is this jasper a good doctor?" Longarm asked.

"When he's sober."

"What's his name?"

"Doc Burnside."

"Tell us how to get to Little Eden and we'll go after him."

"The Elder Booth may not let you take him," Sally said.

"This elder the one needs your water?"

She nodded.

"Then don't worry. He'll see things our way. How do we get there?"

Sally told him. When Longarm was sure he had the directions straight, he turned to Harry. "Let's go," he said.

As Longarm opened the door to step outside, he glanced back to see Sally at the stove, bent over a pot of boiling water. He knew how bad she must be feeling and he wanted to say something to maybe encourage her some. But when he saw the grim, determined resolve on her face, he decided that maybe she would survive without any more words from him. He continued on out through the door and hurried after Harry.

Sally's directions were not difficult to follow. Keeping close by a stream that left the Lazy S range, they lifted their horses to a gallop and kept to that pace during the cooler morning hours. By mid-morning the punishment was beginning to tell on their mounts, so the two men pulled up alongside the stream to let the animals drink their fill and recover their wind. Off-saddling them, the two men slaked their thirsts, then sprawled in the shade of a boulder to rest themselves as their mounts cropped the sparse grass on a flat below them.

Turning to Longarm suddenly, Harry asked how come there were so many Latter-Day Saints hidden away in the Ruby Range. After all, Utah, not Nevada, was Mormon country.

"Maybe so," agreed Longarm, "but Nevada was part of Utah once. Used to be called Carson County, and a pretty big county it was for Brigham Young's Destroying Angels to patrol."

"How come they let go of this rattler's paradise?"

"In Fifty-eight or so silver was discovered here. You've heard of the Comstock Lode, ain't you, and the Ophir? Californians flocked in and began staking out claims. Pretty soon they outnumbered the Saints and demanded statehood, renouncing Brigham Young and all his teachings. There were a few wild rump governments which tried to control the place. The last bunch called themselves Washoes. But it didn't take Lincoln long to see the wisdom of turning Carson County into Nevada Territory. He sent a governor, feller named Nye, to kick out the Washoes and their leader. Pretty soon this here was a free state, and the Mormons already here just stayed on, keeping their heads down and minding their own business."

"It was the silver and gold that did it, then."

"Yep. All them prospectors and miners flooding in here just outnumbered the Saints. Must've disappointed Brigham Young. He had visions of staking his land of Deseret clear to the Pacific."

"Any silver or gold up here in the Rubies?"

Longarm shook his head. "This here's heartbreak country if you're a miner. The silver chloride ore, fairly abundant in the early days, plays out as soon as you dig into it a few feet. But Ely City's into some good stuff, I hear. Course, that don't help anyone up here in the Rubies."

"So what good is this land, anyway?"

"Well, it's dry and it's high. Cattlemen and sheepherders have enough pasture if they can find the water. And it brought you out here to fix up your lungs."

Harry smiled wryly. "It ain't done a very good job of that, Longarm."

Longarm shrugged. "Maybe not, but give it time."

Not long after, they saddled up and left the stream they had been following. Cutting due east in accordance with Sally's instructions, they came at last to a sheer-walled canyon she had told them about. Riding into it, they followed its sandy, brush-covered bottom for a quarter of a mile or so. Then its walls swung wide and they rode out onto a slight rise which gave them an unobstructed view of a long valley spanned by miles and miles of gleaming irrigation ditches. Everywhere they gazed, they saw lush, green fields, each one bordered by a gleaming ribbon of water, the entire valley resembling a multicolored checkerboard. Beyond the fields, on the distant slopes of the valley, Longarm saw clumps of beef cattle, and sheep grazing among the rocks higher up on the slopes.

Longarm was impressed. Little Eden was a remarkable accomplishment which reminded him of other, similar Mormon settlements he had come across in this bleak land.

Spurring their horses on, they followed a wagon trace hugging the steep sides of a bluff. Soon they were riding close enough to the irrigated fields to make out clearly the women laboring through the heat of the midday sun, cultivating the endless rows of corn with small hand-held hoes. Some of the women stood up every now and then to relieve the strain on their backs. When they did so, they watched Longarm and Harry as they rode past, squinting up at them from under the beaks of their bonnets. Their faces were burnt to a wrinkled, leathery brown by the Nevada sun and their eyes showed no curiosity, no light. Watching the women bend once again to their task as they rode past, Longarm could not help but feel that he had gazed not upon women but upon dumb, uncomprehending beasts of burden.

Later, with the fields behind them, the two men topped a slight rise and found themselves closing upon Little Eden. The town appeared to have been laid out with unusual precision, reminding Longarm of Salt Lake City's severe geometry. Most of the buildings in the business district were neatly spaced inside what appeared to be an almost perfect square, with the windmill tower at its center. Surrounding this square on three sides was the residential district, six rows in all of neat houses. Broad avenues ran between them, each one the same distance from the next. Even the outhouses were spaced with tight precision at the right rear corner of each house. And they were just as neat and tidy as the houses.

Separated from the town itself, on a slight rise to the west of Little Eden, the two men spied a large residence constructed entirely of stone. It was surrounded by spacious lawns dotted with cottonwoods; and, if Longarm's eyes did not deceive him, he caught the glint of a large pool in its rear. Beside this impressive mansion there was another residence, a long, low building with curious gabled windows running down its length. If the larger, more imposing structure was the Elder Booth's residence, then the smaller building beside it had to be the elder's *seraglio* housing his many wives.

They left the ridge and followed the trace into Little Eden. Before they reached the town itself, they passed two or three huge warehouses and a mill. Then they clattered over a wooden bridge that spanned a narrow stream, and found themselves passing a hotel, then a restaurant. They kept on until they found a livery stable and cut for it.

They had to drift carefully through traffic heavy with farm wagons groaning under massive loads of wheat and other farm produce. Among these ponderous wagons swept the lighter carts and gleaming carriages of the settlement's businessmen and farmers, their high-stepping horses decked out in as much finery as the carriages themselves. The plank sidewalks were thronged with men and with the many, many women of Little Eden and their children. Each Saint, male and female, was dressed as somberly and as bleakly as their brothers and sisters in Salt Lake City.

35

As Longarm and Harry led their horses into the stable, a young lad appeared out of the gloom and directed them to a couple of stalls in back. After they had taken care of their mounts, Longarm asked the young hostler if he might know of Doc Burnside's whereabouts.

The boy looked at them shrewdly. He was tall for his age, with wheat-colored hair. On his feet were huge clodhoppers heavy with horse manure.

"You two're Gentiles, ain't you?" the kid said.

"Can't deny it, boy," Longarm said.

"You try to take Doc away, we'll have to kill you."

Longarm chuckled and patted the boy on the head. "You just tell us where he is, boy." As Longarm spoke, he flipped a silver coin into the air and caught it.

The gleam in the boy's eyes matched that of the coin. "Doc Burnside's at the Mormon's Rest," the boy said, "sleepin' it off."

Longarm flipped the coin at the boy. "Thanks," he said.

The boy snatched the coin out of mid-air. "I didn't tell you Gentiles nothin'," he said. "Hear?"

"We gotcha, boy. Don't you worry."

They had no trouble finding the Mormon's Rest. It was on the other side of the street, three blocks down from the hotel. From the outside it did not have the traditional look of a Western saloon. There was no false front and especially lacking were the batwing doors, but the tinkling piano and the occasional raucous laughter that exploded from within identified the place unmistakably. Though the two dark-clad Saints ahead of them who ducked inside did so a mite nervously, they went in eagerly enough.

Longarm opened the door and walked inside, Harry following. The place was dimly lit, the floor covered with fresh sawdust, and the mahogany bar ran the length of the room. The rest of the place was taken up by tables and chairs. Along one wall Longarm saw poker tables, their green felt tops gleaming softly in the smoky interior. At this hour of the day the tables were empty. Stairs led to a second-floor balcony. Surprisingly, what with all the women the Mormon males were supposed to have at home, what looked like cribs let off the balcony.

Most of the men crowded into the Mormon's Rest were lost in shadow at the far end and along the walls. As Longarm glanced around, one patron at the far end of the bar, who seemed vaguely familiar to Longarm, pulled the brim of his hat down over his face and hunched over his beer.

"Over there," said Harry, glancing toward a table in the rear.

The fellow Harry spotted as the doctor was asleep, his head slumped forward onto his folded arms, his form partially hidden in shadow, what looked like an empty bottle of whiskey on the table beside him. There was a black instrument bag on a chair near him.

The saloon had gone silent upon their entrance. Now every eye followed them as they strode the length of the saloon and pulled to a halt beside the doctor. The stench of whiskey and sour vomit hung about the sleeping man like a curse. He was snoring loudly. Longarm bent and shook him by the shoulder without gentleness, insistently. At last the man raised his head in protest and glared foggily up at the two men.

"Go 'way," he muttered. "See me later . . . Latimer's Barber . . . office . . ."

Before the man could lower his head again, Longarm slapped him hard. The sound of the slap echoed sharply in the saloon. Everyone in the place came alert. Those at the bar took a step away from it, and the men at the tables got to their feet. Ignoring them, Longarm raised his hand to strike again, but the doctor flung up his hand.

"My good man," he mumbled. "Please. See me later. At the moment, I am indisposed. I assure you, I'll be up and about soon."

"You'll be drunk, you mean," Longarm said.

"You're needed," said Harry. "Now. You must come with us."

"Later, later," the man mumbled woozily as he started to put his head down again. Before he could, however, Longarm tossed his instrument bag to Harry, then hauled Burnside roughly to his feet. Harry glanced back at the barkeep. "You got any coffee?"

"Take more'n coffee to sober up the doc."

"I asked you a question, mister."

"Across the street. Ma's Restaurant."

Burnside tried to pull out of Longarm's grasp, but Longarm hauled the man roughly across the floor. The doctor was stumbling as he kept up with him. As Burnside neared the bar, he reached out and grabbed it.

"Sir," he said, addressing Longarm, his eyes focusing with sudden determination, "unhand me! I am sure I am now capable of proceeding without your encouragement, at least as far as Ma's Restaurant. Perhaps you are right. At this point, a cup of black coffee would indeed go nicely."

Longarm stepped back warily and watched the doctor. The fellow pushed himself away from the bar and squared his shoulders, his red-rimmed eyes bright with determination. Straightening his hat, he managed a jaunty wave to Longarm and walked unsteadily ahead of him out of the saloon, with Harry on his heels.

As Longarm followed Harry down the saloon's veranda steps, he glanced back in time to see a familiar figure stride out of the saloon after him. He was the same gent who had tipped his hatbrim forward so Longarm could not see his face. In the harsh sunlight, Longarm recognized him instantly. He was Sam Connell, the Cross D rider Longarm had unhorsed and set adrift without boots. He seemed to have recovered his fortunes nicely.

As Harry continued on across the street with the doctor, Longarm turned to face Connell. "Howdy, Sam."

"Well, now," Sam said, "if it ain't the Destroyin' Angel."

Longarm smiled. "I never said that for sure, now, did I?"

"Nope. Guess you didn't."

Longarm watched the man carefully, and the others who had followed him out of the Mormon's Rest. In a moment they had packed the porch solid as they waited eagerly for the gunplay to begin.

Sam grinned at Longarm. "I found my boots and got a wagon ride this mornin' into Little Eden, just in time for you to show up."

"Don't try anything, Sam."

"I won't," he assured Longarm. "Not right now. Later. Somewhere on the trail, maybe. Or from the mouth of an alley. Don't worry about when. I'll be the one to decide that."

Longarm turned his back on Sam and continued on across the street to Ma's Restaurant.

Chapter 4

When Longarm and Harry rode into the Lazy S with the doctor at sundown, Sally appeared in the doorway. She looked drained. As the doctor climbed wearily down off his mount, Sally asked them if they had eaten yet.

They all shook their heads. "Didn't think we had time for that," Harry told her.

She pushed a curl off her pale forehead and smiled wearily. "I've just finished baking some bread. Come inside."

As Longarm mounted the porch, Sally looked apologetically at him. "I know it sounds crazy, me baking bread at a time like this. But I had to do something to keep my mind . . . to keep busy."

Longarm put an arm around her shoulder and squeezed gently. "No need to explain. Is there any coffee?"

"Yes. On the stove."

"Thanks. I think the doctor could use some."

As Sally led the doctor inside, Longarm and Harry turned back to see to their horses. When they stomped into the kitchen a few moments later, they found that Sally had prepared a platter full of warm slabs of bread with fresh butter melting on each one. A pot of steaming black coffee sat beside the platter.

As the men sat down to eat, Sally came out of the bedroom and slumped wearily down at the table beside them.

"How's Bill?" Longarm asked.

"He's in terrible pain, Custis. Terrible."

"The doc looking him over?"

Sally nodded.

At that moment Abe and a visibly shaken Doc Burnside joined them at the table. Sally poured the doctor a fresh cup of coffee. He accepted it gratefully and gulped it down. Sally stood beside him, waiting for his verdict.

"Both legs have got to come off," he said.

Sally gasped.

"Gangrene will finish him if we don't," Abe said, reaching out and placing a comforting hand on Sally's forearm.

"I'll need assistance," the doctor went on, looking around the table. "It won't be pretty and it won't be quiet, I am afraid." He glanced at Sally. "I would certainly appreciate something a bit more potent than coffee at this juncture, Miss Sally."

"Afterward," Longarm told him. "You better wait till you've finished taking them legs off."

The doctor shrugged. "You're quite right, of course."

"What will you need?" Sally asked, her voice sounding small and frightened.

As Doc Burnside began to tell her, Abe got up and went back into the bedroom to keep an eye on Bill. Longarm excused himself and left the table to go outside for a smoke, telling the doctor to call him when he was ready. Harry went outside with him.

Closing the door softly, Longarm walked to the end of the porch with Harry, took out a couple of cheroots, handed one to Harry, and lit his own. The two men stood silently on the porch, smoking, each intent on his own thoughts.

Longarm could not help but reflect on the fact that while he was having his way with Bill's wife, Bill was being methodically dismembered by Cross's hirelings. What was even worse was recalling Sally's cruel disparagement, the cold contempt she had heaped on Bill at the very moment he was riding into Cross's compound to call the son of a bitch out. It had been foolhardy bravado, perhaps, but Longarm had to admire Bill for it all the same, while admitting to himself that in a way he had to count himself among Bill's betrayers.

It did not make him feel proud.

The two men were finishing up their smokes when Doc Burnside appeared in the doorway and nodded to them. Longarm flicked his stub into the gathering darkness and followed the doctor back inside, Harry right behind him.

They used the kitchen table. Despite the quantities of raw whiskey they poured down Bill's throat, the man was awake through most of it. At the last, however, the pain was too much for him. He quit screaming and passed out. Burnside hurried then, anxious to finish cauterizing the stumps and stitch over the skin flaps before Bill regained consciousness. The danger was that the doctor might not be able to stop the bleeding. The sound of the hot knife blade searing flesh filled the kitchen.

When it was over, Longarm carried the still unconscious man back into the bedroom, the doctor and Abe following. As he carried the man in his arms, Longarm's heart sank at the difference in Bill's weight. For the first time, it seemed, he was struck with the full impact of what they had just done to the man. Though Bill had not filled his life with triumph and kindliness, he was a man like any other, and this terrible diminution he did not deserve. Longarm felt an icy fury for those who had done this thing to his friend.

When they returned to the kitchen, they found that Sally had disposed of the blood-soaked blankets and what had been left of a grown man's two legs. She was scrubbing the table furiously with a strong soap, its powerful smell serving to clear Longarm's head of the sweet smell of blood. He could see how close to collapse Sally was, but he knew there was nothing he could do or say that could comfort her now.

"Now, Miss Sally," the doctor said. "I'd like some of that whiskey, if there's any left."

Without a word, Sally stopped her scrubbing and went

43

over to the cupboard. Reaching up, she took down a fresh bottle of brandy and four shotglasses. Filling them on the sideboard, she handed a glass to each of them.

Longarm took his glass and gulped its contents down, then went outside. Restless, he left the porch and strode about the yard until he came to a halt finally before a portion of the corral still standing. Leaning back against a charred fencepost, he lit another cheroot and watched the horses cavorting in the pasture beyond the burnt-out barn. Their high-spirited, prancing restlessness seemed to settle him. The horses were sleek, beautiful, their coats gleaming in the moonlight. They were animals that seemed to fit nature's scheme perfectly—unlike man, who seemed always at war with his world and his own spirit.

So far, Longarm reflected ironically, this had been some vacation. He almost found himself looking forward to the soot-filled air and foul alleys, the raucous man-swarm of Denver.

At the sound of footsteps, Longarm turned. The doctor, his face already slightly flushed from the brandy, was approaching him.

"Sir, I'd appreciate one of them smokes, if you'd be so kind," he said.

Longarm handed the doc a cheroot and lit it for him. Burnside looked to be in his late thirties, but it was hard to tell for sure. He had the bulbous, shiny nose of the lush and his lined, sallow face was hollow-cheeked, ravaged. Despite his frailties, however, he had done a better than competent job on that kitchen table. Longarm had seen enough botched amputations to judge. The man was a good doctor. Yet he was swilling his life away in these cruel mountains. And, though Longarm had for years seen men of all sizes and talents doing the same thing, the waste of it, the pure bone stupidity of it, never failed to depress him.

The doctor cleared his throat. "Your friend Harry Wilcox," he said, "has bad lungs. For a while just now, he was coughing some of them out. There was nothing I could do for him."

"I reckon that operation was too much for him."

"For all of us."

"Will Bill be all right?" Longarm asked.

"If Sally can keep the stumps clean."

Longarm took a deep, weary breath and nodded. Sally would be able to do that, he was sure. Through the entire operation she had stood her ground without a murmur. While handing Burnside his instruments, her hands had been as steady as the doc's—steadier, perhaps.

"She'll do it," Longarm said. "It ain't her we got to worry about. It's Bill. I don't contemplate he'll be happy with the view of life he gets from those two stumps."

"You say the Cross D riders did that to him."

"Yes."

"A terrible thing. Terrible."

Longarm could only nod his agreement. "You want me to ride back with you to Little Eden?"

"Mornin's soon enough, if you could put me up here."

"There's plenty of room in the bunkhouse."

"That'll be fine," the doc said. Pushing his shoulders back, he braced himself wearily. "I'd better look in on my patient first," he said, "then get some shuteye. I'm all done in."

"Thanks for coming, Doc."

The man smiled crookedly up at Longarm. "Why, sir, I don't believe I had any choice in the matter."

"I reckon maybe you didn't, at that."

Burnside tossed the stump of his cheroot into the darkness, turned and walked back to the ranch house.

The next morning, with Harry remaining behind with Abe to keep an eye on things, Longarm rode back to Little Eden with Burnside. They both dismounted in front of the Mormon's Rest, and the doc could hardly wait to spend his fee as he scrambled up the steps of the saloon and pushed inside.

Longarm followed cautiously in after him, eyes narrowed, alert. Pushing up to the bar, he continued to look around. Sam Connell was not in the place. It was early yet, Longarm realized. Sam would be in soon enough, once he heard Longarm was in town.

"Bottle of whiskey," Longarm told the barkeep.

The fellow slapped a bottle down before him, a shotglass by its side. As Longarm drew the bottle toward him, he studied it curiously. "This here's whiskey?"

"It'll do," the barkeep told him.

"What is it?"

"Valley tan."

"That's Mormon whiskey."

"Where the hell do you think you are, mister?"

"Nevada, one of the United States."

The barkeep moistened his lips nervously and glanced around the saloon at the now silent, staring faces. Then he looked back at Longarm. "It's valley tan or nothing. You don't like it, leave."

Short of holding up the place so he could search for a bottle of good rye whiskey, there was not much Longarm could do. With a shrug, he turned and started from the place just as the door opened and Sam Connell strode in.

He was not alone. Behind him was a small party of dark-clad Saints, one of whom towered over the others. He had a long white beard that extended halfway down his chest and icy green eyes that peered out from under beetling brows. His mouth was a grim, unforgiving line.

"That's him!" cried Sam, pointing at Longarm.

The tall fellow nodded curtly. He signalled with his hand for those with him to remain where they were and strode up to Longarm. Reaching him, he smiled coldly at Longarm, his eyes alert.

"I am Elder Booth," he said.

"Pleased to meet you, Elder."

"You've brought back Doc Burnside, have you?"

"That's right."

"Real neighborly of you. This cockroach behind me said you represented yourself to him as one of my riders. That so?"

"It seemed to impress him," Longarm said.

"And now he wants to join my band. I have you to thank for that."

Longarm shrugged.

"You are staying at the Lazy S. That right?"

"I am."

"And what do you find there so interesting, besides Bill Adams's wife?"

"That's a long story."

"Come to my place and tell it. I have plenty to drink there. Good whiskey. Not this poison."

"We could talk here."

The elder's smile went cold. "No. My place. Come willingly or those men behind me will bring you. They will not be gentle."

"So it's your home, then."

"Yes."

"You have whiskey, you said. Any Maryland rye?" Longarm asked.

"Of course."

"Why didn't you say so in the first place?"

The elder's palatial stone mansion was even more impressive close up. The cottonwood-shaded lawn was expansive and meticulously kept; and it cooled everyone off wonderfully as they rode in the elder's carriage through the trees to the mansion. As Longarm left the carriage on his way to the massive stone steps leading to the front entrance, the elder's guard close behind him, he managed a quick glimpse to his right and saw that there was indeed a pool behind the house.

It was enclosed in arbors and evergreen shrubs, with the elder's *seraglio* on the far side of it. For an instant, Longarm thought he heard the laughter of women splashing in the pool.

A bottle of Maryland rye was produced as soon as Longarm was made comfortable in the elder's cool, almost cavernous living room. The elder poured for both of them. Longarm thanked the elder with a salute, after which the two men downed their whiskey.

At once, the elder got down to business, asking Longarm for an account of the Lazy S's recent difficulties, as he put it, with the Cross D. Longarm saw no reason for denying the man what information he had and told him all he knew, finishing up with an account of Bill's present condition.

As Longarm leaned back to let what he had told the elder sink in, the only sound he heard was that of the grandfather clock's pendulum swinging solemnly in the far corner of the room. The elder had refilled his glass and was sitting in a high-backed Morris chair, a troubled frown on his face.

"This man Cross is a greedy man," he said at length.

"Yes."

"He wants land."

"Yes."

"And he wants water."

"You know better than anyone, Elder. Them two items better go together up here."

The elder leaned back in his chair, his alert eyes studying Longarm carefully. "You are a dangerous man, Long. What that cockroach Connell has told me about you convinces me of that. And the way you came in here for Doc Burnside proves it. You are a man who likes to take direct action, and I'd guess there's not much you'd let stop you, once you got the bit in your teeth."

"What's on your mind, Elder?"

"What are you going to do about the burning of the Lazy S and the maiming of your good friend, Bill Adams?"

Longarm shrugged.

"Surely you plan on doing something," the elder persisted.

"Of course."

"What?"

"That's my business, Elder."

"But you *will* do something. You won't just stand idly by and let Cross get away with such a violation of your friends. Am I correct?"

"Get on with it, Elder. What are you driving at?"

"Just this. What happens to the Lazy S happens to Little Eden as well. The water on which the Lazy S depends for its survival is the same water we ourselves need. Bill and Sally Adams have been very generous in sharing that water and have assured me that as long as they own that spread, we will not have to worry. The dam on their land dividing the flow of water so that I may feed this valley will not be disturbed by them. That is their promise, and I believe they will keep it—as long as they can. But Dalton Cross may not let them keep that promise. As you said, he wants water."

"What do *you* want, Elder?"

"I do not want you to oppose Cross openly."

"You mean you want me to sit back and let Cross have what he wants."

"Yes. At least for now. I am hoping I can make some kind of an accommodation with the Cross D. Any action by you, though certainly justified, might be enough to unleash him and his entire force of gunslicks—not only on the Lazy S, but on Little Eden as well, with drastic results no matter which way it went."

"How do you figure that?"

"Cross has an ace in the hole. Friends in the governor's office. If it came to a battle for that water and we defeated him, his political patrons would doom us. We would be pictured as fanatical Mormons who had destroyed a prosperous rancher whose only fault was attempting to gain water for his stock. If we lose in the battle and his men

49

succeed in cutting off our water supply, we must pick up and go elsewhere. And there *is* no elsewhere for us, Long."

"So you're going to deal with Cross."

"If I can."

"And that means dealing away the Lazy S."

"If that is what it takes."

Longarm got up. "Not on your life."

"Please. Sit down. Think it over. Finish your drink."

"Sally and Bill Adams are my friends. I don't have to think it over." Longarm put down his glass and strode for the door.

Before he reached it, the door swung open and a grinning Sam Connell, four heavy-set bruisers on his heels, stepped through it. The four were carrying bung starters and seemed eager to put them to use.

Behind him, Elder Booth said, "Longarm, meet four members of the Danite Band. I advise you not to struggle. They will not deal with you gently if you give them trouble—and that, I assure you, is precisely what that cockroach with them would like."

For an instant Longarm considered going for his Colt, or perhaps his derringer. But it was far too late for gunplay now. He had already blundered too far into the spider's web.

"All right," he said, turning back to Booth. "There's no need for any of this. I'll do as you suggest. I'll hold off."

Leaving his chair, the elder walked over to Longarm with what appeared to be sincere regret on his face. "It's no good, Longarm. I'd be a fool to accept that promise now. You have made your intentions perfectly clear, I am afraid. I shall have to confine you until I have met with Dalton Cross."

"And then?"

The big man shrugged. "We will cross that bridge when we come to it. I am sure Dalton Cross will deal with me if I am able to throw the Lazy S into the pot." He smiled. "Meanwhile, Long, relax. I will see to it that you are made

50

quite comfortable, and that you have a goodly supply of Maryland rye to console you."

Abruptly, the elder's smile vanished. He stepped back, his sharp glance fixing on the tallest of the four men. "Take Long to the restraining room. Unless he gives you trouble, I do not want any harm to come to him. That's an order."

As the men surrounded Longarm and nudged him from the room, Longarm saw the elder hold Sam Connell back. Connell seemed pleased at the special attention—and did not mind at all, it seemed, that the elder continued to refer to him as a cockroach.

The door was kicked shut behind Longarm, and he was led off.

Chapter 5

As soon as Longarm was alone in the elder's restraining room, he became aware of the sound of women splashing about in water. It came from close by—just beyond the room's outer wall, he reckoned. There was only one window. It was barred and made of stained glass. Looking closer at it, he saw where a portion of the stained glass had fallen out of its lead border. Pulling a chair over, he stepped up onto it and peered out through the tiny opening.

All he could see was a portion of the elder's garden enclosed by thick hedges and junipers. Shifting his chair to bring him closer to the window, he managed to change his angle of vision. This time he saw not only the elder's pool but the elder's many wives cavorting in its cooling waters, and not one of them encumbered by a single stitch of clothing. In the privacy of their concealed garden, they evidently considered themselves secure from prying eyes.

It was a sight to make a grown man sweat. Unlike most of the rest of the Mormon female tribe, these young ladies—most of them in their early twenties—were quite lovely, their heavily-bosomed figures having already blossomed into full womanhood, their faces radiating a mischievous and happy vitality. He counted twelve in all, an even dozen. Longarm shook his head in wonderment. He wished Billy Vail could be here to see this. Never in his life had Longarm seen such a rich abundance of female breasts bobbing about in the water.

Only two of the women were not frolicking in the water. One was asleep on a comforter on the grass. The other—easily the most beautiful, with long, wheat-colored tresses, high cheekbones, and eyes like patches of blue sky—sat quietly under a tree, hugging her knees as she gazed broodingly at the others. Occasionally those in the pool would pause in their play to call to her, but she shook her head somberly each time. They called her Kristen. It occurred to Longarm that this one might be a recent initiate into the elder's harem and might perhaps be having some difficulty accepting her new status.

Longarm watched her for a while, then pulled back from the barred window to give his fevered imagination a rest.

The restraining room, as Elder Booth had called it, was in the basement of the *seraglio* itself. Though comfortably furnished with table and chairs, an upholstered divan, and a large four-poster bed, it was a damp and not very cheerful cell, especially when Longarm considered the four sets of chains that hung from the walls. Judging from the sizes of the neck and ankle collars, they were fashioned for women, undoubtedly those young ladies of Elder Booth's harem who occasionally needed restraining.

Longarm heard footsteps, followed by a sharp knock on the door. The key rattled in the lock and the door was pushed open. One of the men who had escorted him to this room entered, carrying a box. Without a word he set it down on the table, turned, and left.

Longarm walked over to the table and opened the box to find that Elder Booth had kept his promise. Rye whiskey. Longarm chuckled grimly to himself. The elder was not being generous. He was hoping Longarm would drink himself into a stupor, which would sure as hell keep him out of mischief.

Longarm left the bottles of whiskey on the table and retreated to the upholstered chair. He slumped into it, his brow furrowed, his mind racing. His ass was in a sling, and

54

no matter how well-upholstered the sling, he wanted out—not whiskey.

After a while, he glanced thoughtfully back at the bottles, then got up and walked over to the window. After studying the hole in it for a while, he broke off a leg from one of the chairs and used it to break out more of the stained glass. As he worked, the shrill cries of the women splashing about in the pool effectively blocked out any noise he made. When he thought the hole was large enough, he poked the wooden leg out through the hole and waggled it slightly until he saw the blonde sit up suddenly, staring in his direction.

Pulling the leg back out, he called, "Kristen!"

She narrowed her eyes, then looked quickly about her to see if anyone else had heard. Satisfied, she looked back toward the window.

"Come closer," he called, "to the window."

She tipped her head slightly as if considering his request, then glanced carefully around a second time. Satisfied that no one else was paying any attention, she rose to her feet. It was a sight that made Longarm catch his breath. Her blonde pubic hair gleamed like cornsilk between her ample thighs. Without the slightest appearance of haste, she walked around the edge of the pool, pausing once or twice to talk briefly to a few of the splashing women. Once past the pool, she kept going until she was standing in front of the window.

Turning her back to it, she called softly, "Who are you?"

"My name is Long," he told her, addressing her small, firm buttocks. "Custis Long. I'm in the restraining room. Do you know it?"

"Yes," she snapped. "I know it."

"Help me get out and I'll help you."

"Are you younger than the elder?"

"Yes."

"Your voice is strong, vibrant. I will believe you. But if you are lying, I will not help you."

"Agreed."

"Tonight. After midnight. I will come to you then."

She walked back to the pool, skirted it as before, then sat back down, again hugging her knees. But this time, Longarm noticed, there was color in her cheeks, and her gaze was no longer so melancholy.

Longarm tried to remain awake, but exhaustion claimed him and it was not until the door closed behind his visitor that he came awake. So dark was the room that he saw only a pale, ghostly form coming toward him.

"Kristen?" he whispered.

"Yes. Do not light a lamp."

"I can hardly see you."

"We shall let our hands see for us both." She was so close to him now he could smell the heat of her, the indefinable perfume of her hair and body. He flung back the covers and sat up, reaching out for her at the same time.

Her nightgown melted from her pale form, becoming a shimmering puddle at her feet. She stepped closer and came easily into his arms. He spread his legs and she kept moving toward him. When his solid erection nosed gently against her pubis, she sighed, leaned back, and with her hands on his shoulders, shoved forward. She was already moist and he slipped into her with lovely ease. Still sighing, she leaned back, working his shaft still deeper into her.

He pulled her hard against him and she let her head rest on his shoulder, her long hair cascading down his back as she held him. Reaching down, he caught her under the thighs, then stood up quickly. She grunted with delight and crossed her legs behind his back, her thighs digging into his waist. He felt his shaft thrusting still deeper into her, wondering why she didn't cry out. Instead, she muttered with pleasure and hugged him still closer.

He began to turn around, then spin.

"Oh, my!" she cried softly. "You *are* much younger than the elder. Don't stop! Don't stop!"

Still turning, he laughed and said, "Not yet, I won't."

He kept on spinning, faster and faster, while she hung on, delighted, her head thrown back, laughter pealing from her like music. At last, dizzy and exhausted, he plunged for the bed and, with her under him, came down on it with explosive impact. Keening sharply, she tightened her arms about his neck, her strong thighs scissoring him as she leaned hungrily back, pleading with him to go still deeper.

But he didn't need her to tell him that. He commenced to plunge into her with a recklessness that set him to growling hungrily. With each savage thrust, she let loose with a powerful, deep-throated grunt. Before long they were hurling themselves at each other like two infuriated animals locked in combat. He surged toward the edge, then plunged over, taking her with him until at last they collapsed, panting fiercely, in each other's arms.

After they caught their breath, she nibbled his earlobe and whispered, "Who in the hell *are* you, Mr. Long?"

"A damn fool who just got himself between a rock and hard place."

"I guess that's me, too."

"You don't like being a member of the Elder Booth's harem?"

"I do not." She dropped her hand to his crotch and began playing idly with his large tool. "For one thing, he is too old to tend to his obligations properly. And when he does, he does *not* please."

"Well, honey, *you* sure as hell know how to please."

"Thank you, Mr. Long." She sighed, still gently massaging him. "I must admit, I have been aware of the pleasures of the flesh for some time—from when I first realized how attractive I was to the opposite sex, I am afraid. It had been a marvelous ten years—until I arrived at this place."

"How old are you?"

She had him coming to attention down there, and his loins were beginning to throb in anticipation. "Twenty-six."

"How'd the elder get hold of you?" He tried not to think of what her fingers were doing to him.

"Don't you know about his night riders?"

"The Destroying Angels?" Sweat was standing out on his forehead.

"I don't know what they're called for sure. All I know is they wear hoods and they ride by night, ranging far and wide for his harem." As she spoke, her educated fingers were running lightly up and down the back of his erect, straining shaft.

"Go on," he told her, writhing in delightful agony as he buried his face in her snowy breasts.

"Anyway," she went on, her voice like music in his ears, "them night riders didn't have to work hard to get me. In Ely City I was delivered up to them bastards by a man I trusted. A gambler. He needed some money to pay off a debt and made a deal with the riders. It seems the old bastard had heard of me and sent those men to get me." She closed her arms tightly about him, almost smothering him in her breasts. "So here I am."

She had driven Longarm nearly crazy by this time. Asking no more questions, he pulled her roughly up onto him. Laughing happily at the prospect, she spread her long legs and straddled him, leaning close to kiss him on the lips, her fragrant canopy of hair falling over his head and shoulders. Then she reached back with one hand and guided his erect shaft smoothly into her as she sat back. He felt himself slipping in and closed his eyes.

She began to move slowly back and forth, gradually increasing the tempo. He leaned back and closed his eyes and let her govern the pace. At last, when she had aroused him to a feverish pitch, she laughed gently and slowed, bringing him back down again carefully, still rocking gently back and forth. Then, slowly, she increased her tempo.

But enough was enough.

Reaching up with both hands, he fondled her breasts roughly, then drew her down to him. While his thumbs flicked at her nail-hard nipples, he began kissing her deeply, passionately. Soon she was answering him in kind, her darting, reckless tongue sending electric shocks deep through him, clear into his vitals. Unable to hold back any longer, he pushed her roughly back, grabbed the blades of her hips, and began working her savagely up and down his shaft. Laughing, she reached forward and grabbed his hair to have something to hang on to as they both swept over the edge.

A long time coming, they finished up clinging drunkenly to each other as their convulsive shuddering gradually subsided. At last, groggy and light-headed, he allowed her to roll off him; they were both covered with a fine glaze of perspiration.

Snaking her arms around his neck, Kristen kissed him on the cheek lightly and said, "You did not lie. You *are* much younger than the elder, and much stronger, too, I think."

"Maybe. But after that, I'm not so sure."

She laughed softly.

"You mind telling me how you managed to get in past the guards?" he asked.

She smiled, and her blue eyes lit mischievously. "You mean you *really* don't know?"

"Well, I just wondered if that was it."

Chuckling, she let her finger trace a light path down his belly. "Your guard's name is Matthew," she told him. "He is very big and very solemn and whenever we start undressing him, all he can say is, 'Oh, my! Oh, my Lord!' Two of the girls are with him now down the hall. Soon he will be on his back, snoring. He always goes to sleep afterward."

Longarm grinned. "Then this ain't the first time."

"Of course not."

"The poor son of a bitch is going to lose his job if he gets caught."

"He'll lose more than his job. And it won't be so pleasant for the girls, either. But that doesn't matter. You have no idea how much we all hate the elder. He is a vicious, cold man. It takes forever to get him up, and when we do, he

59

makes us feel dirty for being with him." She shuddered involuntarily. "For weeks after, you feel unclean, crawly."

"I get the picture."

She peered at him closely. "All right, Mr. Long, you said you wanted my help to get out—and that you would help me get out also. Remember?"

"I remember."

"What's your plan?"

"Get me out of this room, for openers."

"That is easy enough. I have the key. But after that? What then? There are other guards all around the compound. The elder calls them his Guardians. You won't be able to leave without one of them catching you."

"So what we need is a diversion."

She smiled and propped her head on her elbow. "Exactly."

"There's a case of booze over there on the table. Good booze. The best. Maryland rye. I suggest you deliver it to the rest of the elder's harem. It's about time the girls got something better than valley tan to tickle their tonsils."

"The elder would be furious if any of us got drunk."

"The cat's away. It is time for the mice to play."

"Booth is away? You know this for sure?"

"He's gone to meet Dalton Cross—to hatch mischief, I have no doubt. He rode out with a few men right after he locked me up in here."

Kristen sat up quickly, her eyes suddenly gleaming with excitement. "I see what you mean, Long! The girls could perhaps share all that lovely whiskey with their keepers— if, as you say, the cat's away."

"The night is young. Do you know any who might appreciate a whiskey of this calibre?"

"Hell, yes. A damn sight more than one. Where's the liquor?"

"On the table over there."

She got up and reached down for her nightclothes. "Get dressed and be ready. I'll see to the rest."

As she vanished back out the door, Longarm lit a lamp and dressed hurriedly. It was after midnight, yet he felt as fresh as a robin. He had to be careful not to move too quickly, however, for fear he might sail over the furniture, so light did he feel.

Three girls returned with Kristen. One look at the rye whiskey and they uttered tiny shrieks of delight. With Kristen helping, the three lifted the box and vanished back out through the door. Longarm could hear their excited laughter as they moved off into the *seraglio*. Kristen returned soon after, fully dressed.

"Listen," she said, her eyes gleaming mischievously.

Longarm cocked his ear. The women's laughter was much shriller now, more heedless. Glass shattered, followed by more shrieks of laughter. Then came the heavy tread of booted feet clambering up the stairs and entering the building.

With a quick frown, Longarm glanced at Kristen.

"Our guards," she said, smiling. "They were invited to join the party."

Grinning back at Kristen, he said, "Let's go."

In back of the elder's mansion was a small, solid building constructed entirely of stone that served as the armory for Little Eden. It was in this building, before riding off with Sam Connell to the Cross D, that the elder had had Longarm searched thoroughly.

Longarm tried the armory door. It was not locked. He pulled it open and stepped inside. Lanterns hanging from nails high on the walls illuminated the barrels of gunpowder and the long wooden boxes of rifles and ammunition piled high against the walls. The elder had enough firepower in this one building to take over half of Nevada, Longarm realized. The cool, damp air of the place fell over him like a blanket as he and Kristen moved carefully along, keeping close to the wall.

61

Ahead of him was the room where he had been stripped of his weapons. The door was closed and there was a light under it. As they got closer to it, he thought he heard sounds of low laughter and giggling coming from it, which meant the guard on duty was not only enjoying the elder's whiskey, but one of his women as well. When Longarm and Kristen reached the room's doorway, they flattened against the wall and listened. From within came the sound of a woman's laughter, soft and coaxing, as she urged her man on.

Kristen smiled.

"It is Marie," she whispered. "She's always liked this guard. And he could never take his eyes off her."

"How romantic," said Longarm. "But right now both of us are helpless until I break in there and get my weapons. Go back outside and keep a watch."

"I could help."

"You could help by going back outside and warning me of anyone's approach."

She shrugged. "As you wish."

Longarm waited until Kristen was outside, then kicked the door open and stormed in, reaching the wall rack containing his Winchester before the guard was able to roll off Marie. Swinging the rifle barrel like a club, Longarm caught the man on the side of his head. He flopped over, unconscious.

"Get him out of here," Longarm told the woman. "Fast!"

Whimpering with shock, Marie snatched up her undergarments with one hand, the guard's leg with the other, and dragged him from the room.

Longarm found his saddlebags, rig, and Colt hanging on a peg on the wall. He had seen one of the guards stash his derringer and watch in the desk drawer. Pulling it open, he was pleased to find them still there, including a handful of cartridges. After a quick inspection of his firearms, he grabbed up a couple of boxes of .44-.40 and left the room, taking the kerosene lantern with him.

Striding to the rear of the armory, he held the lantern

high and saw boxes of explosives and ammunition piled high against one rear wall. He hurled the lantern. It shattered on impact, and there was a loud *whump* as the kerosene ignited, then sprang up the side of the boxes. Longarm ran from the armory.

As he closed the door behind him, Kristen stepped from the shadows. "Did you get your weapons?"

He showed her the Colt and patted the derringer in his vest pocket. Eyes gleaming, she took out the derringer and hefted it. "My, but you are a sneaky one, Mr. Long."

"Them two gone now?" he asked her, looking warily about.

"Yes," she said, placing the derringer back into his vest. "My God, Long, what did you do to that poor guard?"

"Never mind that," he told her. "We'd better make it to the stables before this place goes up!"

They ran across the dark lawn, heading for the big horse barn. They had almost reached it when the armory went up with a shattering explosion. As if a giant hand had picked them up, they were both flung forward onto the ground. Night became day as a series of tremendous concussions continued to shake the ground under them. Scrambling back up onto their feet, they ducked behind a corner of the barn. Two men rushed from the wide-open stable door, shielding their eyes from the glare. The men took one look and ducked back into the barn for buckets, then bolted back out again, heading for the burning armory.

Slipping into the stable with Kristen, Longarm found his own mount, saddle, and bedroll. He saddled up swiftly, then helped Kristen saddle the horse she had selected. Ducking their heads low, they rode out the rear of the stable.

As Longarm turned his mount toward Little Eden, Kristen called, "This way!" and headed toward a slope that loomed out of the night well to the east. "There's a trail through the mountains up there! It'll take us around the settlement!"

"How do you know?"

"One of the guards told me," she called back. "He was

going to take me with him."

Longarm could believe that. Kristen was obviously not one to let pass any opportunity to get out from under Elder Booth's tyrannical hand. She had probably been ripe for a breakout the moment the elder brought her to this place, and Longarm was lucky he had found her before she made her move.

Looking back, he saw men and women rushing through the blazing darkness toward the still thundering armory. Going back that way, through that swarm of furious Mormons, would have been suicide.

He turned his mount and spurred after Kristen into the darkness.

Chapter 6

They were well into the foothills before they realized they were being pursued. As they broke over a ridge, a rifle cracked from the darkness behind them and Kristen's horse collapsed under her. She managed to throw herself clear, but the animal was done for, thrashing feebly in the darkness, trying desperately to lift his head.

Longarm flung himself from his mount, snaking his Winchester from the scabbard as he did so. Kristen raced over beside him.

"Them bastards!" she cried, glancing back at her horse, tears tracing a path down her cheeks. "Let me have your gun!"

He unholstered his Colt and handed it to her, mildly surprised. She slipped down the slope to the horse and ended its misery with one well-placed shot.

As she ducked back down beside him, handing him the Colt, Longarm saw the first horseman break out of a dark patch of rocks and cross a patch of pale, moonlit ground. A moment later, two more dark, flitting shadows followed. Despite the darkness, they were riding as if the hounds of hell were on their heels. And maybe they were. These were probably some of the elder's special Guardians, trying desperately to make up for their dismal performance so far this evening.

Maybe it was the rye whiskey still buzzing about in their heads, but they rode straight on at the slope, making no effort at concealment. Sighting carefully on the closest rider, Longarm squeezed off a shot, bringing him and his horse down. The remaining riders, realizing too late how exposed they were, split up. Longarm cranked in a new shell and downed a second rider. By this time the third one had vanished into a dark clump of pine.

Longarm turned to Kristen. "Let's go," he told her. "That last one won't be so anxious to follow us now."

"I don't have a horse."

"We'll just have to ride double."

"Can your horse manage that?"

"If we take it easy," he told her, mounting up.

He reached down. She hiked her skirt up as far as it would go, then took his hand and mounted up behind him, snaking her hands around his waist. As he spurred his mount on up through the dark foothills toward the pass she had told him was there, she leaned her cheek against the hollow of his back and hung on.

The pass was where she said it would be, and once through it they dropped rapidly through twisting gullies and arroyos toward the distant flats gleaming in the moonlight far below them. Before dawn they were out of the foothills and made a dry camp, sleeping until the sun came up. When it did, it revealed a long, desolate salt flat extending to the southwest, a rugged mountain chain to the north, and the Ruby Range at their back.

Longarm figured that if he went south, keeping close to the Rubies, he would find a way back through the range to the Lazy S. He was anxious to get back. Though he knew Harry was with Sally and Bill, after his chat with Elder Booth, he realized there was bad trouble brewing for the Lazy S.

They ate a cold breakfast of beans and hardtack, all that was left in Longarm's bedroll. As he kicked sand on the fire and peered reflectively back at the jagged ridges they had probed down through the night before, Kristen approached him, leading their one mount.

"Ely City is across that flat," she told Longarm. "We'll need water to get across."

"We ain't going across that flat," Longarm replied. "We're heading southeast, back to the Lazy S. On the way I'll leave you off in Ruby."

"No, Mr. Long," she told him sharply. "I want you to take me to Ely City. If I stay here in the Rubies, the elder will find me again and bring me back. Besides, I have a score to settle with the son of a bitch who sold me to Booth."

"Then stay with me until we get to the ranch. You can go to Ely City later."

"I'm going now," she said.

As she spoke, she hiked her dress well past her hips and swung into the saddle as deftly as an Indian. Swinging the horse around, she lifted it to a lope.

"Come back here, damn it!" Longarm called after her in pure exasperation. "You'll never make it across that flat!"

"Yes, I will!"

He took out his Colt. "You heard me!"

Glancing back, she saw the firearm gleaming in his hand, and laughed. "You won't shoot me!" she called back. "You're too much of a gentleman!"

She clapped her heels to the horse's flank then and lifted the horse to a gallop.

"Wait!" he cried, honestly alarmed for her safety by now.

She kept going a while longer, then turned the horse and reined it in. Brushing her long golden hair off her shoulder, she sat still for a moment on the horse and looked coolly back at him.

"Are we going southwest?" she called.

Longarm was licked. She held all the cards. Without a horse he would be crowbait in less than a day. Already the sun was boring a hole in the back of his neck. "All right!" he called to her, holstering his Colt.

"No tricks?"

He didn't answer. It was bad enough he had to give in. He didn't want to have to lie as well. She hesitated a moment longer, studying him carefully. Then she spurred the horse back toward him.

As she slipped down beside him, she smiled. "I'm glad you're a man of your word," she said, "or I wouldn't have ridden back for you."

"For a lady, you're pretty tough, ain't you?"

"I never said I was a lady, Mr. Long."

"True enough," Longarm admitted, swinging into his saddle and reaching down for her.

She swung up behind him again, clasping her hands around his waist. Her right hand, he noticed, was damn close to the butt of his Colt. As he lifted the horse to an easy lope, he realized he was going to have to be very careful with this one.

Four more horsemen appeared on the ridge above them just as they got done filling up their canteens at a water hole before they reached the flats. Kristen was ducking her head into the water hole, and when she popped her head up, blowing like a seal and rubbing her eyes, he pointed them out to her.

"Recognize any of them?"

She peered through the morning glare and shook her head. "They're too far off."

"You still want to try to make it across that flat to Ely City?"

"Yes. We've got a good start on them."

"Once they get through the foothills, they'll make good time on that flat."

"I say we stop arguin'," she told him, squeezing the water out of her hair, then brushing it quickly back.

Longarm pulled the horse away from the water hole and mounted up, Kristen slipping up behind him now with practiced ease. Turning the horse, Longarm started across the salt flat, heading for a low pile of mountains shimmering in the distance. In the midst of that crumpled rampart was Ely City, about the last real boom town left in Nevada. It

68

looked like a full day's ride—and it had better not take any longer than that.

He looked back to the ridge. It was empty, which meant the riders were already picking their way down through the tortuous arroyos and canyons toward them. By noon at the latest, they would have reached the flat. Longarm turned back around. Kristen's arms tightened about his waist, her cheek resting once more against the small of his back.

A few hours later they dismounted in among a monstrous pile of rocks to give themselves and the horse a much-needed rest. The rocks towered incongruously in the immensity of the alkali flat, their surfaces dark and highly polished. As Longarm studied them, he was reminded that this enormous flat had once been the floor of a vast inland sea, with these same rocks thrusting up through the surface, perhaps. He could almost imagine the restless waters passing over and through this pile of rocks, smoothing and polishing them, while gulls and giant sea birds of another age rested upon their backs.

Climbing to the top of the nearest rock, Longarm peered back through the searing heat and thought he saw their pursuers, their dark, mounted forms trembling and shimmering in the heat, their horses seemingly walking on air. He clambered down to where Kristen was resting.

"They're coming up on us," he told her.

"How far back?"

"It's hard to tell."

"How many?"

"Still four."

"I say we wait here for them and take their horses."

"There's four of them, and only two of us. I don't like the odds."

She shrugged and got to her feet. "Let's go, then."

They did not stop again until they reached an upthrusting of rock that again offered them some relief from the merciless rays of the sun. It was about half a mile before a wide, dry river bed, the gravel in it polished to such a bright sheen by flood waters that even at this distance neither of them could look directly at the wash without squinting. It was the middle of the afternoon, and the ramparts toward which they were heading still hung tantalizingly before them on the horizon. The four riders on their tail had long since disappeared behind them, and it was a good bet they had given up, the sun was so hot by now.

That was the good news. The bad news was their horse. He was in bad shape. His chest was streaked with dried lather and his eyes were inflamed from the windblown alkali.

Longarm unsaddled the horse. Dampening his handkerchief with water from his canteen, he squeezed it out onto the animal's lips and tongue, repeating the process until the horse was able to accept tiny doles of water directly from the canteen. When the horse had finished up what water was left in it, Longarm hobbled him and let him graze on the sparse patches of salt weed growing in among the rocks.

"How much farther is it?" Kristen asked wearily. Her eyes were bloodshot and her lips cracking from the alkali also. Longarm himself had been riding with his bandanna up over his nose and his hatbrim pulled well down over his forehead. It had helped some, but not much.

"I figure we'll make the mountains by nightfall."

"We don't seem to be getting much closer."

"I know. It's the heat. Raises hell with anything sitting on the horizon."

"You must hate me."

Longarm shrugged.

"I just have to get back to Ely City," she explained. "Noplace else is safe for me."

"Maybe if you had asked me instead of . . ."

"You mean if I had begged. You had that look in your eyes, Mr. Long, the one most men get when they've made up their mind."

70

Longarm shrugged. It was foolish to waste time discussing it now. Kristen slumped wearily back against the boulder to protect herself against the sun and dozed off as Longarm gazed at the dark hump of mountains in the distance. He was not really as certain as he had sounded to Kristen when he told her they would make it across this flat before sundown.

About fifteen minutes later, Kristen stirred and sat up. Like Longarm, she had noticed how strangely chill it had become. They looked to the north and saw a long black curtain of cloud moving across the sky like the wing of some stupendous bird. Then Longarm heard the distant muttering of thunder as, deep in the black bowels of the cloud, lightning gleamed with the swiftness of thought. Abruptly the wind changed direction. Wicked dust devils swirled tiny grains of sand up into their faces. At the same time, the sudden chill grew in intensity, as if they had been flung into a cool root cellar.

He glanced at Kristen. She was shivering. "My God, Longarm," she said. "It's getting *cold*."

"Storm coming."

Longarm went over to the horse and brought it back to them so he could keep it from spooking when the storm hit. Pulling the horse around so its rear was facing the wind, he took off his suit coat and flung it over the horse's head. Then he removed the slicker from around his bedroll and flung it over both of them. By this time the swirling wind was flinging dust and rock shards into their faces with cruel effect, forcing Kristen to duck her head against Longarm's chest to protect herself. Holding her close, he moved nearer to the horse.

Not five minutes before, the blistering heat had had Longarm wringing wet with perspiration. Now the storm's sudden, icy chill had him shivering violently. Thunder cracked overhead. Holding the horse close to steady it, Longarm glanced up. The black cloud they had seen approaching was now moving over them. Behind it, white cottony tendrils were hanging down, some reaching clear to the desert floor. Peering into the cloud's flickering darkness, Longarm saw a dark, hazy curtain being dragged along the surface of the flat.

Rain. And lots of it.

"Here it comes," Longarm told Kristen. "Get ready."

She just shivered and clung more closely to him.

There was a sudden crash of thunder, this time accompanied by a blinding bolt of lightning, then another, and still another as the thunder came in a series of deafening detonations barely seconds apart. Keeping pace with the bone-jarring crashes was the constant play of lightning which kept the ground around them bathed in an eerie, bluish glow.

But Kristen saw none of this, so close was she clinging to Longarm. The horse, its head down, was trembling violently from head to tail, uttering a kind of groan as Longarm kept his right hand over its neck to hold it close.

Then came the rain. Longarm heard it crashing upon the ground as it swept toward them, sounding like someone had opened an enormous faucet. The first heavy drops struck at them like whip lashes. Then came a solid, battering downpour. There was no mercy in it whatsoever. It felt like someone upstairs was emptying buckets onto them. Raindrops pounded him like buckshot, plastering the slicker to his back, drumming furiously on his hat, causing solid rivulets of water to pour off his hatbrim.

By this time, the relentless, lashing tendrils of rain were causing Kristen to gasp out in shock and pain. Longarm bent his head and shoulders over her, taking the brunt of it, as the rain continued to thunder down upon them. But soon, like her, he found himself gasping to catch his breath. It was as if they were both sinking under water. It was only when he thought he could take no more that, as swiftly as it had overtaken them, the rain swept on, slackening to a steady, pounding downpour that was almost a caress after what they had just endured.

Drenched through to the bone, Longarm stepped away

from the horse and saw that the water in the wash ahead of them was rising fast. He looked around, blinking the rain out of his eyes, trying to see through the steady rivulet draining off his hatbrim. The lightning had let up also and the thunder was now only a dim, fretful muttering in the distance.

"My god," Kristen said, shivering violently. "I thought I was going to drown."

He nodded grimly, then pulled his suit coat off the horse's head and flung it over his shoulders. He gave his slicker to Kristen and a moment later she struggled up behind him on the horse. With their heads down, their shoulders hunched against the relentless downpour, they started toward what had been a dry wash. By the time they reached it the black, silt-laden water had already surged up past the horse's fetlocks.

They pushed out into the water, struggling against the current, which became swifter and more powerful with each passing second. Halfway across, the water was up past the horse's knees, and by the time they reached the far bank, the water was brushing Longarm's stirrups. Once their horse dug its way powerfully up onto the far bank, they halted and glanced back.

"Longarm! Look!"

But Longarm had already seen them. The four horsemen they thought had given up on them were looming out of the shifting curtain of rain on the far side of the stream. Wearing their slickers, as the four riders approached the bank, they looked like great, misshapen birds.

Dismounting quickly, Longarm snaked his Winchester out of his saddle scabbard and glanced up at Kristen. "I don't think they can see us through the rain," he told her. "Ride on. I'll wait here for them and catch up to you later."

"Alone?"

"Don't argue. Ride on, damn it!"

Kristen scooted forward onto the saddle and, using the reins, lashed the horse on into the dark curtains of rain.

Horse and rider disappeared into the gloom, the steady downpour drowning out any sound from the horse's hooves.

Ducking low, Longarm tucked his rifle's breech under the skirt of his coat and trotted downstream until he found a sodden ridge of cheat grass and mesquite close by the bank. He flopped down behind it for cover, a sudden gust of rain slamming behind him on the back so heavily that he almost lost his breath.

By now the horsemen were crowding the far bank, evidently reluctant to chance the rising current. Then one of them moved out into the water and was immediately followed by the other three. Almost at once their horses were up to their chests in water and began drifting with the current as they struggled to make headway. By the time the first rider gained the near bank, less than twenty feet from where Longarm was lying in wait, the rest were strung out downstream, struggling desperately to make headway.

Longarm waited until the three stragglers gained the bank and were riding up to join the lead rider. Then he stood up to cover him with his rifle.

"Tell your friends to stay put!" he shouted at him through the pounding rain. "Do it, or I'll blow you off your horse."

"You heard him!" the horseman called frantically to the others.

The horsemen behind him pulled their mounts to a halt and Longarm strode quickly closer to the nearest rider. "Dismount," he told the Mormon. "And don't make any sudden moves."

As the rider complied, one of the riders behind him muttered angrily, flung back his slicker, and went for his sixgun. But the skirt of his slicker slowed him fatally. Longarm shifted the rifle and fired. The bullet caught the fool in the chest and knocked him back off his horse.

The other two horsemen broke back into the water. One let his horse carry him downstream, while the other—in a superb example of horsemanship—turned his horse about in the raging waters and moved back across the surging torrent. In a moment, both riders were out of sight.

Longarm swung his rifle back to cover the first rider, who was standing beside his horse, the rain beating on him mercilessly.

"Unbuckle your gunbelt and let it drop," Longarm told him.

The man did as he was told. Longarm strode forward through the driving rain and kicked the gunbelt into the swirling waters. Then Longarm took the reins from the rider and swung into the saddle.

"You son of a bitch," the Mormon said, glaring up through the rain at him, his nose dripping pathetically. "That's one of the elder's best horses!"

"Tell him I appreciate the loan of it."

"You can't leave me here like this!"

"Why, sure I can," Longarm said, dropping his Winchester into the saddle scabbard. "That won't be no trick at all."

"Damn you, mister! You tell that bitch we'll get her. And you, too!"

Longarm spurred the horse, making no effort to avoid the irate Mormon. At the last moment he leaped aside, landing face down on the puddled ground. His cries were lost in the downpour, and Longarm did not look back.

In half an hour or so the drenching rain had become a drizzle that gave way finally to a steady shower. The thunder was only a barely audible mutter, the lightning just occasional flashes that lit up the belly of the storm clouds moving on to the southeast. The hoofprints of Kristen's horse were not completely wiped out by the rain, and as the late afternoon sun came out and the world rapidly dried, the trail she left across the flat became no chore at all to follow.

She was not sparing the horse, Longarm noted, and not once did she slow down to see how he was doing. It was obvious she had no intention of circling back for him. Like a good, sensible girl, she was looking out for number one.

This woman would never lose a buck or her life through an overdose of sentimentality, he realized wryly.

He left the flat behind an hour or so before sundown, and as night fell his horse was lifting him into wooded foothills. Coming upon a stream, he decided to make camp. He was about to dismount when he heard a gunshot from his right. The bullet hummed past and he turned in his saddle to see one of the riders he thought he had left at the wash galloping toward him from a stand of timber not fifty yards away. The hard-charging rider fired a second time before Longarm could haul his rifle from its scabbard.

He levered swiftly and fired. The hammer came down on a wet cartridge. He levered and fired a second time, but again his bullet failed to detonate. Another bullet whistled past him, this one tugging at his left sleeve as it burned a hole through it. Dropping the rifle, Longarm reached across his belt for his Colt. Before he could bring it up, however, the rider was on him, his horse slamming violently into Longarm's, sending both men toppling from their saddles.

Longarm landed heavily, the other rider coming down behind him. As Longarm flung himself about, he saw the rider up on one knee aiming his Colt point-blank at Longarm, a grim smile on his wild, bearded face. Here was a Latter-Day Saint who took his orders seriously, Longarm thought as he flung himself desperately to one side.

There was a sudden thunder of hooves, so close that the ground under him shook. Then came a man's terrified scream that was cut off abruptly. Longarm looked back to see the Mormon on his back, a great, jagged hole in his chest. Beyond him, Kristen was wheeling her mount to return for another run at the downed rider.

"Enough," Longarm told her, getting to his feet. "He's done for."

She pulled up close beside Longarm and gazed down at the man she had just run down, her eyes gleaming in triumph. "I know him," she said. "He was the one tended to us when we spent time in that restraining room. The dirty son of a bitch really enjoyed his work."

Longarm bent over the man, examining the hole in his chest. The hoof had broken through the Mormon's rib cage, crushing his heart.

"We better move on," Longarm told Kristen. "There's probably more where this one came from."

She shook her head and dismounted. "I been watchin' since you left the flat. This one was the only rider following you. He kept abreast of you in the hills. I figured if I rode down to warn you, that would only make both of us a target. Trouble is, he came at you a little sooner than I thought he would."

"Never mind that. You did the right thing. I owe you."

She looked at him shrewdly. "You helped me get out of Little Eden. Just now I saved your ass." She smiled. "That right?"

Longarm nodded.

"So that makes us even," she went on.

"I suppose it does."

"Then I'll take the Mormon's horse and you can have yours back. I can get to Ely City from here easy enough. And you can ride back to your friends. If that's what you want."

"That's what I want, Kristen."

"Good. But first I suggest we find another camp site and sleep under the stars. Together."

He chuckled. "We should both be very tired."

"Why, Mr. Long! Too tired to make love?"

"Sometimes the spirit is willing, Kristen, but the flesh is weak."

She shrugged. "We'll see."

They camped higher in the foothills, with fragrant pine boughs under Longarm's soogan, the clear night sky above, and a soft wind flowing like water through the pines. Longarm found that with the aid of Kristen's expert talents, his flesh was more than a match for the spirit.

Chapter 7

Two days later, cutting through the Rubies on his way back to the Lazy S, Longarm came upon a high meadow dotted with flocks of sheep. He pulled up to let his horse blow while he watched a single black and white border collie nipping at the heels of a few strays on a nearby slope. Thoroughly engrossed in watching the collie, he let his guard down. The clink of iron on stone alerted him. Swinging around in his saddle, he saw a Basque sheepherder nudging his small Indian pony out from behind a huge boulder, the bore of his shotgun aimed at Longarm.

"Put away the cannon," Longarm told the man. "I'm no threat to you."

"Who you ride for?"

"The Lazy S."

Slowly the man lowered his shotgun. "I have not seen you before this," he said. He was a short, powerfully built individual, his eyes black slits in his face, his expression impassive. He wore a wide-brimmed sombrero, and over one shoulder rested a multicolored wool serape.

"Just rode in a few days ago," Longarm replied.

"You come to help Miss Sally?"

"Her and Bill."

The Basque looked closely at Longarm, his eyes questioning, hard. "I wish I may believe what you say. That you are for the Lazy S."

"Why is it so hard to believe?"

"Cross. Son of a bitch, he bring in many new riders. All with bright sidearms. He want all this land. He is one greedy man."

"You think I might be one of his gunslicks?"

"Maybe."

"Ride with me to the Lazy S. See for yourself."

He gestured with his head to the sheep carpeting the meadow. "I must tend my flock. If not, I go with you, for sure." He tipped his head. "How are you called?"

"Name's Long."

For the first time the man smiled, his white teeth flashing brilliantly in his dark face. "That is a good name for you. I am Diego. Tell Miss Sally I stand with her against Cross."

"Just you?"

He smiled thinly. "There are many Basque in these mountains. They are loyal to me and we come to stay. You tell Miss Sally that."

Longarm touched the spurs lightly to his horse's flanks. "I'll do that," he said.

The Basque pulled his horse back and dropped his shotgun into his saddle sling. When Longarm topped a rise a moment later and glanced back, he saw the Basque scattering sheep as he rode across the meadow, heading for a cluster of rocks high on a ridge. Longarm could not be sure, but he thought he saw another sheepherder waiting for him in among the rocks. When he caught the glint of sunlight on binoculars, he was sure.

He turned back around and kept on over the rise.

Early the next morning, well inside the Lazy S range, Longarm heard the soft pound of hooves on the trail behind him. Turning, he saw Abe following him at a respectful distance. His rifle butt was resting on his pommel, his left hand raised in greeting. There was a grin on his face.

Longarm pulled up to wait for him.

"You're getting a mite careless, looks like," Abe remarked as he pulled alongside Longarm.

80

"Hell, I thought I was on friendly range," Longarm told him as he and Abe rode on together.

Abe chuckled, then sobered. "What took you? You been gone a while. Miss Sally and that friend of yours're gettin' a mite edgy."

"I was visitin'. Elder Booth was kind enough to extend his hospitality to me. It was very interesting."

Abe did not know what to make of that, so he said nothing.

"Where you comin' from just now, Abe?" Longarm asked.

"The north range. Sally wanted me to check out the stock and the water hole and make sure that dam is still in good workin' order."

Longarm was heartened by this news. It looked as if Sally was taking charge nicely. "How's Bill?"

"Bad. He don't like what's happened to him."

"Can't say as I blame him."

"And the worst of it is, Miss Sally's keeping him cold sober."

Longarm could see the wisdom of that, but also the problems it might be causing. It was bad enough losing both legs, but having to stop drinking at the same time would be pretty tough on a hard drinker like Bill.

"Just met one of your neighbors, Abe," Longarm told him.

"Who might that be?"

"Diego."

The old cowpoke made a face. Sheepmen still were an offense to his cowpoke sensibilities. "That Basque sheepherder," he said, nodding. "He throw down on you, did he?"

"Like you say, I'm getting a mite careless."

"He moves like an Indian, that one. His native tongue ain't anything I'd care to wrap my tongue around, either. Sounds worse'n a drunken Ute."

"He says he's on our side."

"He ain't got no choice. Cross is just as anxious to move

in on Diego's grazin' land as he is to take over Lazy S."

"How much help do you reckon he'd be, if it turns out we need it?"

Abe let fly a gob of tobacco juice. "Ain't no doubt of it. He'd be plenty help, him and the rest of his people. They hang as tough as ticks on a grizzly."

By that time the Lazy S ranch house was in sight. Longarm spotted Sally and Harry in the front yard, both of them dragging away lengths of charred timbers from the site of one of the burnt-out barns. They were working so hard they did not notice Longarm or Abe until the two riders left the ridge and started across the swale toward them. It was Sally who saw them first. She seemed delighted to drop what she was doing and call over to Harry.

"Where you been, Custis?" she demanded as he dismounted beside her. "I thought maybe you'd run out on us."

"You know better than that."

She smiled suddenly. "That's what Harry said."

Harry was standing beside her. "I knew you'd be back," he said, grinning. "She did, too. Sally just wants to needle you."

"I met the elder," Longarm said. "And one thing led to another. But that'll come later. You had any visitors since I been gone?"

"It's been peaceful enough," said Sally. "But I'm worried. I know Cross is up to something."

"How's Bill?"

The question put a sudden damper on things. Harry looked at Sally. She took a deep breath. "He's not good, Custis. He just lies in that bed, looking at the spot where . . ."

" . . . the bedclothes kind of fall away to nothing," Harry finished for her. "He ain't takin' it good, Longarm."

"How else could he take it?" Longarm asked.

"What they mean," said Abe, "is Bill's gettin' mean. Real mean."

"All right. I'll go in and see him."

They kept behind him as he entered the bedroom. Longarm saw a bearded, scruffy-looking caricature of the man he had known as Bill Adams. His face was shrunken, his eyes bloodshot. He greeted Longarm with a surly wave and asked him what the hell he was doing back here, since Harry was now on hand to service his wife.

In the shocked silence that followed, Longarm leaned over and slapped Bill in the face, hard.

"Custis!" Sally cried, aghast.

Bill massaged his red cheek and looked up at Longarm with blazing eyes. For a moment, he tried to lift himself to swipe back at Longarm.

When he fell back, unable to manage it, Longarm smiled. "Good," he said. "If I can get you mad enough, maybe you'll stop feeling sorry for yourself. The only reason you thought you could get away with a crack like that is you thought no one would dare strike a cripple."

"Damn you! That's a lie!"

"Is it?"

"You know damn well it is. I was just callin' it like I saw it. And you know I speak the truth," Bill said.

"Maybe. But that's beside the point right now."

"What do you mean?"

"You got to get out of this room, stop feeling sorry for yourself." Longarm paused, looking reflectively down at Bill. "What do you think, Bill? Would you feel any better if you could get back on a horse?"

"Sure I would. But how the hell could I manage that?"

"I'm not sure. But I think maybe it could be managed."

Bill looked away. "It ain't no use. You're just trying to shake me up. But it ain't no use. I ain't a man no more. I'm a freak."

"Let's get out of here," Longarm said, turning to the others.

Shocked at his cold-blooded manner, Sally and the others nevertheless shuffled out of the room ahead of him. Longarm slammed the door behind him and led them into the kitchen. He indicated the table with a sweep of his hand, and once they were seated, he turned to Abe. "I want you to get a wooden chair and put wheels on it. You think you can do that?"

Abe thought a moment, then looked at Longarm. "Well, I know where I can get me a set of wheels."

"Abe," Sally suggested eagerly, "what about that rocker in the back shed?"

"Just the thing," Abe said, brightening.

Longarm nodded. "That'll do it, then. We'll let him stew in there a while, then take him outside and plant him in a wheelchair under that cottonwood, whether he likes it or not."

Sally smiled at Longarm, relief flooding her face. "I think he *will* like it, Custis!"

"What you said about him riding a horse again," Harry said. "You really think he could manage that?"

"Hell," broke in Abe, "I've seen redskins on horseback with no legs at all. But then there ain't nothin' could keep an Injun off a horse, to my way of thinkin'."

Longarm looked around the table and spoke quietly and earnestly. "Once Bill gets his strength back and finds his backbone, anything's possible. We'll put together some sort of rig to hold him in the saddle. But right now, the thing we got to do is get him the hell out of that bedroom."

There was no argument to that.

The next morning, bright and early, Abe brought out the wheelchair he had fashioned overnight and set it down under the big cottonwood shading the front yard. He was obviously quite proud of his handiwork, as was Harry, who had lent a hand. Sally softened its rough contours with blankets, then brought out some old magazines and placed them in the deep, lush grass beside it.

Longarm waited until Bill had finished his breakfast before striding into his room. Bill had turned on his side and was staring at the wall. He turned irritably to gaze up at

Longarm as he paused beside the bed.

"What the hell do you want?" Bill demanded.

"Thought you might like to get out of this bedroom."

"Sure. I'd like to fly, too." Bill looked away from Longarm and down at the spot where his legs should have been. "No problem at all. You just wait a minute while I get up and dress. Be with you in a minute."

Longarm reached down and flipped the blanket off Bill, then lifted him up in his arms. "We've got a chair outside for you," he told the man. "Under the cottonwood."

A pine jay uttering an agitated *shook, shook, shook,* darted like a crazy blue lightning bolt out of the cottonwood as Longarm set Bill down carefully in the wheelchair. It was a clear, fresh morning with the dew still heavy on the grass under the tree, and it promised to be a fine day. In the repaired corral beyond one of the ruined barns, a horse whinnied exuberantly.

Longarm stepped back.

"How's that, Bill?" Harry asked.

Harry was standing with Sally and Abe, hoping, like the others, to see a smile at last on Bill's sunken, almost cadaverous face. But Bill seemed determined to disappoint them. He glanced ironically at his wife.

"Guess it'll be a whole lot easier for you now with me out of the house. Ain't that right, Sally?"

Bill's ugly insinuation was clear to all. Longarm felt his face flush in indignation, but he held himself in check. After all, the poor son of a bitch was right. Longarm looked grimly away from Bill's distorted face in time to see Sally, tears exploding from her eyes, turn quickly and run back into the house. Harry, about to go after her to give her some comfort, thought better of it and held up, glancing uneasily at Longarm.

"Let's go, Harry," Longarm said. "You too, Abe. I'd like you to show me that water hole and dam everyone's so anxious about."

With obvious relief, the two men followed Longarm as he strode away from the cottonwood and the sullen, legless man in the makeshift wheelchair.

It was close to noon when they rode into a stand of timber, the wind sighing hauntingly in the tops of the pines. Ahead of them through the trees, Longarm could see the high, lush north pasture. Breaking from the pines, he glanced up at the towering, white-capped peaks beyond—and, closer to them, the canyon inside which Bill and Sally had constructed a dam.

Leading them across the high pasture and into the rocks, Abe took them still higher, to the rim of the canyon above the dam. Longarm dismounted and walked to the edge of the canyon rim, looking down at the earthen dam Sally and Bill had constructed in the canyon's mouth, which caught the stream flowing into the canyon. Looking down, he saw the water backed up through the entire length of the canyon, forcing it to spill out the far end and giving Little Eden its year-round supply of irrigation water. Meanwhile, the water rushing over the log spillway into a broad, meandering stream was what fed the Lazy S water holes and the meadows and parklands beyond.

Without this dam, then, only the barest trickle of water would reach Little Eden, and the Mormon community would be doomed.

"I've seen enough," said Longarm, mounting up.

They were heading through a light stand of pine not long after when the three riders heard ahead of them the sound of brawling, unhappy cattle. As they kept riding, they saw through the trees a broad sweep of pasture, and moving across it a huge cattle herd. They could also hear the whistling and shouting of the drovers hazing the beef on.

Abe pulled up quickly and glanced at Longarm. "Them ain't our cows," he told Longarm. "And them ain't our hands drivin' them, 'cause we don't have any. Besides, I choused the northern herd onto the lower slopes yesterday."

"So whose are they?" Harry asked.

"Cross D, more'n likely," said Longarm, dismounting swiftly.

Pulling his Winchester from its scabbard, he led the two men through a patch of undergrowth to the timber's edge. On their bellies, pushing cautiously through the brush, they saw below them a large herd of cattle being driven toward one of the Lazy S's water holes. As they watched, the frantic brutes piled into the water so many ranks deep that the cattle in the rear could not get through, while those in front were already floundering in water up to their necks. Their frantic bawling filled the dust-laden air with a massive bleat.

Behind them the high pastureland had been cut up cruelly, revealing dark clods where the plunging hooves had sliced open the turf. Behind the cattle, a ragged band of riders continued to push the cattle relentlessly, seemingly intent on driving the poor thirsty creatures mad. But gradually, as the cattle managed to surround the hole and nose their way into the water, they quieted down somewhat.

"At this rate," said Abe bitterly, "there won't be nothin' left but a mud hole."

"No question those are Cross D riders?" asked Harry.

"No question."

As the three watched, the drovers, having completed the drive, rode over to a clump of pine and dismounted, letting the animals drink up. They were an untidy, motley group, each one heavy with sidearms. For such men, Longarm reflected, the task of driving a herd of cattle this high into the Rubies must have been quite a chore.

"You think they might try to take that dam?" Abe asked Longarm.

"They don't have any reason to. Looks to me like a deal's already been struck."

"Between Elder Booth and Cross?"

"Right. This here is their way of letting Bill and Sally know they don't have any more say on this range. They've been squeezed out."

"Like hell," muttered Abe as he levered a fresh cartridge into his rifle. "I'll blast their asses all the way back to Hades."

Longarm rested his hand on Abe's shoulder. "Calm down, Abe. Don't get your bowels in an uproar. First off, I only recognize a few of them riders down there. You want to help me out some?"

"That big one," Abe said, pointing, "the fellow sits his horse like a gorilla, he's Sledge, Cross's bully boy. He ain't bright enough to get in out of the rain, but he takes orders, especially when it means a chance to stomp someone. The one beside him is Burt Hoover, and Lem Shanks is squatting alongside him. The others're new to me. But that don't mean nothin'. Cross has been bringin' in hardcases for the last couple of months."

"So what're we goin' to do?" said Harry.

"I told you," said Abe. "Blast the bastards!"

"Now hold on," counseled Longarm. "Just hold on a minute. Let's get back into the pines and eat this here apple one bite at a time."

Once in the pines, they hunkered down to parley. Longarm had a plan he thought might work, but before he could say more than a few words, Abe let his rifle down into the tall grass beside him, startling a covey of bobwhite chicks. At once they exploded into flight, fluttering and scolding in all directions. The panic was contagious. In the branches high above their heads, a flock of crows suddenly took flight, cawing indignantly.

At once the men realized this might alert the Cross D riders to their presence. "I better take a look," said Abe.

"I'll do it," said Longarm.

A moment later, he poked his head through the brush and peered down at the Cross D riders. They were all on their feet, staring up the slope in Longarm's direction. As

Longarm watched, Sledge said something to a man still sprawled on the grass. The fellow got to his feet reluctantly. Sledge raised his voice and the rider caught his horse's rein and swung into the saddle.

Longarm pulled back through the brush. "A rider's on his way up here to investigate."

"Should we cut him down?" Harry asked.

"I say we take him," said Abe.

"My thoughts exactly," said Longarm. "But we've got to do it real quiet. Get over there in those bushes," he told Abe, "and let me handle this. Harry, get behind that tree over there."

"What're you gonna do?"

"Watch and you'll find out."

As the two men vanished into cover, Longarm dropped his hat to the ground, then took out his handkerchief and let it catch onto a small bush beyond where he'd dropped the hat. This accomplished, he ducked into a thick clump of willows close by the handkerchief.

The Cross D gunslick, his head down to clear the branches, was soon pushing his way into the timber. Unwilling to dismount, the rider nudged his horse into the small clearing and pushed his hat back off his forehead, a bored, unconcerned look on his bearded face. It was plain that he did not take this errand very seriously.

But as soon as he saw Longarm's hat lying on the ground, he came alert. Dismounting, he hurried over to pick it up. Then he looked quickly around and spotted the handkerchief. As he was reaching for it, Longarm moved out silently from the willows behind him, holding his Colt over his head, ready to bring it down on the back of the man's skull.

Harry began to cough.

It was a raw, hacking sound that caused the rider to spin around, clawing frantically for his gun as he did so. Still a few feet from the man, Longarm flung himself upon him, burying his shoulder in his mid-section, feeling the sudden expulsion of breath as the man went reeling back. A tree trunk slammed into the back of his head. His eyes rolled back and he collapsed unconscious to the ground

"That wasn't very pretty," said Abe, stepping from cover, a grin on his face. "But it sure as hell got the job done."

"Sorry about that, Longarm," said Harry, still holding a handkerchief to his mouth. "I tried not to cough, but it got the best of me."

"Forget it."

"Now what?" Abe said.

Longarm studied the unconscious man, then glanced up at Harry. "This gunslick looks to be about your size, Harry."

"So what?"

"Get into his vest and pants and put his hat on. Then ride back out of the timber. They'll think it's this fellow here. Wave them on up here. They won't suspect anything, and we'll be on them before they can respond."

"You hope," said Abe.

"Yes, I do," said Longarm.

Abe grinned suddenly. "Don't worry. We will."

Dressed in the unconscious man's hat and vest, Harry rode out of the timber, fired his Colt to catch Sledge's attention, then sat astride his horse and waved to Sledge and the rest of the Cross D riders. As soon as they were all mounted up and rowelling furiously up the slope toward him, Harry vanished back into the timber.

According to Longarm's plan, Harry pulled his mount to a halt alongside the unconscious, nearly naked gunslick on the ground and slumped forward over the pommel, his face hidden from the Cross D riders spilling into the pines. When Sledge saw the unconscious gunslick on the ground, he flung himself from his horse and knelt quickly beside him.

The moment he turned the man over and saw who it was, he looked up in some confusion at Harry—and found himself staring into the bore of a sixgun.

"Tell your boys to drop their gunbelts, Sledge," Harry said.

Sledge hesitated.

"Do it or you're a dead man."

From the bushes came a shot. A rider to the left of Harry settled sideways off his horse, his revolver falling from his hand. There was something in the way he settled on the ground that told every man watching he was dead. Abe stepped out of cover, his Colt smoking. Cocking the side-arm, he took cool aim on Sledge.

That did it.

"Drop your gunbelts, boys!" Sledge cried. "We're sur-rounded!"

The men did as they were told. Harry and Abe swept up the sidearms and tossed them back down the slope. Then Longarm stepped into the clearing and directed the Cross D riders to dismount. As soon as they had done so, he told them to take off their boots.

This command shook them. They looked uncertainly at each other, then back at Longarm. Sledge spoke up then. "There's just the three of you, ain't that right?"

"Looks like it," said Longarm.

"We can take you if we got a mind to."

"Try it."

He was a big, hulking fellow, with a shock of unruly, jet black hair, a broad, heavy forehead, and a punched-in, flattened nose. His jaw looked like it had been chiseled out of granite and there was no excess tallow on his six-foot frame.

"We ain't takin' our boots off," he announced.

Abe fired at the ground in front of the nearest man. At once the Cross D rider began tugging off his boots, and his companions hastily followed his example.

All except Sledge.

"I don't care what they're doin', no one's takin' my boots off," he told Longarm suddenly, his head lowered like a bull ready to charge.

Suddenly he hurled himself at Longarm. The sheer force of his charge was enough to rock Longarm back. When

Longarm pulled up and tried to bring up his sixgun, he felt Sledge's numbing paw slam into his hand, knocking the weapon from his grasp. Still Longarm held his ground as he felt Sledge's battering fists numbing first his left cheek, then his shoulder. Rocked back on his heels, he fought to stay up, returning Sledge blow for blow, his knuckles cracking painfully against the big man's forehead and chin, then sinking deep into his gut. For a full minute the two men stood toe to toe, exchanging brutal, sledging punches, until the telling, efficient precision of Longarm's blows began to rock Sledge steadily back.

Longarm saw the man begin to swing more wildly, with a reckless, almost feline fury that at times left him wide open. Gasping for air, his arms now almost as heavy as anvils, Longarm swung on him, sending slashing blows to Sledge's head and neck. He saw Sledge stagger repeatedly but refuse to go down. Longarm rushed him, mixing it up brutally, his fists crunching on the man's nose, ripping at his face and neck. Sledge sagged to one knee under the fury of the onslaught, and Longarm drove in to finish him off. But, amazingly, Sledge lurched upright and flung himself head down at Longarm, catching him in the gut. Reeling backward, Longarm's heel caught on a root, and suddenly he was on his back, staring woozily up at a patch of blue sky.

Before he could gather his wits, Sledge had buried his boot into Longarm's kidney. Sharp, excruciating pain swarmed up his side as Sledge staggered back to aim another kick at Longarm's head. But Longarm was ready this time. Reaching up, he grabbed Sledge's booted foot and twisted violently. Sledge went down hard, the back of his head slamming into the ground. In a second Longarm was on his feet. He aimed one kick at the side of Sledge's head and the man flopped over and lay still.

Stepping back while he sucked in deep gutfuls of air, Longarm ordered one of Cross's riders to take the bastard's boots off.

Finally, when all the boots had been collected into a pile, Longarm had them buried under tinder, the ground around the pile trenched and filled in with rocks. Then he dropped a lighted match on the pile. A thin trace of smoke showed first, then vanished as a bright yellow flame flared up. In a moment the flames were racing through the small bonfire, devouring the boots.

Sledge stirred groggily.

"Get him up," Longarm told the Cross D riders, "and take care of that other one," he added, pointing to the unconscious rider he had slugged earlier. "Then move on down this slope. We'll keep your mounts. You got a long walk ahead of you before you get back to the Cross D, so you better start now."

"You can't do that," whined a still groggy Sledge. "You can't make us walk all that way barefoot—not over all that stony ground!"

Another man protested, "That ain't human!"

"Guess maybe you're right," Longarm told them. "It ain't. But I'm doing it anyway."

Abe unlimbered his sixgun and sent a couple of rounds into the ground at their feet. The men scrambled back, turned, and began hobbling down through the timber, some of them slipping comically on the slick pine needles.

"Sledge!" Longarm called.

The big fellow turned.

"I got a message for your boss. Tell him if the Lazy S can't use this here water no one else is going to, either. No Gentiles and no Mormons."

Sledge frowned.

"Repeat that, Sledge."

The big fellow repeated Longarm's words just as Longarm had spoken them.

"Now, git," Longarm told him.

The three men watched the forlorn gunmen straggle on tender feet down through the timber to the flat, then skirt the herd still milling about what had become—as Abe had predicted—a huge mud hole.

Mounting up, Longarm and his two companions rode down to the flat, circled around behind the milling cattle, and began firing over their heads. Already pretty well spooked, the cattle let loose with shrill bleatings and began climbing over each other in the frantic desire to get away from the blazing sixguns.

Though some of the Cross D cattle never did escape the water hole, the vast majority churned back across the water, scrambled up the muddy, torn fabric of the bank, then stampeded across the flat and from there on down the slope. The Cross D riders had to scramble some to keep from being trampled, but Longarm did not worry about that as he and the others galloped past the bootless, unhorsed gunslicks and kept the plunging cattle on the move.

A good mile or so farther on, Longarm pulled up to watch the seething torrent of backs and horns vanish into a broad canyon that Abe assured him led eventually onto Cross D land.

"That message," Harry said, pulling his horse to a halt beside Longarm, "the one you gave Sledge to take back to Cross. What did you mean by that?"

"You mean you don't know?"

Abe, patting the neck of his sweating horse, glanced shrewdly at Longarm. "What you meant was we'll blow that dam if they don't leave us be."

Longarm nodded. "That's about it, Abe."

"But, hell," said Harry, "you talk like that and they may move first and take the dam away from us."

"Let's say I'm inviting them to try."

"You're talkin' war."

Longarm shrugged and pulled his mount around. There was no need to admit the obvious.

Chapter 8

A day later, Dalton Cross was standing on his porch talking to Pete Walsh and Jeeter when he caught sight of the long, weary line of unhorsed gunslicks plodding through the noonday sun toward the ranch compound.

"What the hell," he said, stepping down off the porch. "If I didn't see this with my own eyes, I wouldn't believe it."

Pete Walsh grinned, his big hand rubbing the hard black stubble on his jaw. It made a harsh, scraping sound in the still, hot air. Jeeter smirked.

"Wipe off that smile," Cross snarled at Jeeter. "This here ain't funny. I was wondering where the hell they were. They been gone all night."

Jeeter sobered instantly. "You think the Goshutes mighta done this?"

"Them diggers'd never attack a man on horseback. You know that."

Cross strode angrily across the yard to meet his men. Sledge was in the lead, and when the big man pulled up in front of Cross, the owner of the Cross D noticed not only Sledge's bloody feet, but his battered face as well. Looking around at the rest of the men, he noted their condition.

"Who did this?" Cross demanded.

"That man Long, the one who's throwed in with the Lazy S."

"You mean *he* did this?" Cross demanded, incredulous. "All by himself? One man?"

"He wasn't alone," Sledge replied sullenly, brushing his sweat-heavy hair back off his forehead.

"What you mean is Sally Adams was with him. That it?"

"No, Mr. Cross. Her hired man, Abe. And that lunger, Harry Wilcox."

"So it took three of them, did it? Three of them to unhorse you clowns and send you back here barefoot!"

"They caught us by surprise."

"That so? With fools like you, I wonder why they bothered."

"That ain't fair, Mr. Cross," protested Sledge.

"Damn you! I'll tell you what's fair and what ain't."

Sledge nodded respectfully. "Yes, sir."

"I'll send some hands out after your horses. It would help some if you'd tell Jeeter here where you saw them last and which way they was headed."

"There's something else," Sledge said, licking his dry, cracked lips nervously.

"Out with it!"

"That big feller, Long. He told me to tell you that if the Lazy S can't use that water, nobody else could either. Then he said something funny. He said no Gentile or Mormon."

Cross swore softly and surveyed his men. By this time they were all inside the compound, drawn up alongside the miserable, hulking Sledge, who kept his head down so as not to meet Cross's furious gaze. There were eight men in all, the best guns he could hire, imported from every hellhole in the West—each one, he had been told, with notches on his gunbutt. Now they stood uneasily before him, downcast, woebegone, a lineup of losers who had been routed as well as humiliated by this fellow Long and two other men who, before this time, Cross wouldn't have thought worth a pinch of coon shit.

"Get out of my sight!" he told the men wearily. "And if any of you want your time, I won't stop you."

Spinning on his heels, he strode angrily back to the main house, Jeeter and Pete Walsh scurrying after him, neither willing to resume the conversation they had been having when Sledge and the others showed up. At the porch steps, Cross halted and turned to face them.

"You go see Cookie if you're hungry. Pete, I'll see you later. We got some talkin' to do."

"You're damn right, Cross," Pete Walsh said. He was a long, lean, sharp-eyed man in his thirties, with dark hair and clean, polished features. Dressed in his dark trousers and frock coat, his white shirt still gleaming after the long ride from Ely City, he was a startling contrast to his late brother. "Ham and I, we didn't get on all that good, but he was my brother. I want the son of a bitch who killed him."

"We both do, Pete."

"Jeeter mentioned a thousand dollars if he brought me back."

"And another thousand," Cross reminded him, "when you kill that son of a bitch. We'll talk about it later."

Turning abruptly, Cross continued on up the porch steps and went inside his big living room, where Elder Booth was still waiting patiently. As soon as Cross relayed to the elder the message Sledge had just delivered to him, the elder asked for another whiskey, a request which accurately conveyed to Cross the depth of the Mormon's concern.

After pouring the elder's whiskey, Cross turned to the squat, pan-faced Goshute woman waiting in the doorway. "Coffee," he told her. "Then something to eat."

She vanished.

"Sit down, Booth," Cross said. "We got some plannin' to do. Seems like the Lazy S is declaring war on both of us."

With a weary sigh, the elder slumped into an easy chair.

A couple of days later Elder Booth, flanked by six dark-clad riders, rode into the Lazy S compound and found one of the barns partially rebuilt. Basque sheepherders were

97

wielding hammers with a vengeance. Bill Adams was sitting in a crude, makeshift wheelchair under the cottonwood, a double-barreled Greener in his hands.

Pulling his mount to a halt, Booth rested his hands on his saddle horn. "Glad to see you up and about, Bill."

"Who the hell says I'm up and about? What do you want, Booth?"

With a soft word to his men, Booth dismounted and walked across the yard toward Bill. "Now, why're you so riled at me, Bill? I ain't the one put you in that chair."

"No, but you're in bed with the bastard who did."

Booth glanced warily around. The Basque sheepherders had put down their hammers and saws, replacing them with rifles and sidearms. The assorted weapons were of various sizes and bores, even one flintlock, but they gleamed brightly in the sun and looked quite serviceable.

Then Booth saw two horsemen, Abe and Harry Wilcox, pulling to a halt behind his men. A second later a third mounted rider came into view, a rifle resting across his pommel. Long. That son of a bitch, Long. The man who had spurned his hospitality, despoiled his women, and destroyed his armory. For an instant Booth looked as if someone had opened a door on the arctic, so frozen with malice did his face become.

He turned angrily on Bill. "Put that shotgun down, Bill. You ain't actin' very hospitable."

"Say what you got to say, Booth, then git."

"You got to see it my way. I need to be sure of my water source. The Lazy S is finished, and you might as well admit it. That leaves just me and Dalton Cross to settle the water rights up here. I have no choice. I must throw in with Cross."

"You could have throwed in with us," Bill Adams replied coldly.

"You're in no condition to fight the Cross D, Bill. Haven't you noticed? They cut you off at the knees."

Bill swallowed. The elder's bluntness had been deliberate, an obvious attempt to shake Bill into an awareness of the hopelessness of his position. But it seemed only to have goaded him to a quiet, menacing fury.

"My guts ain't in my feet," Bill told Booth tightly.

Sally came out of the ranch house then, wiping her hands on her apron. She regarded the elder coolly. Booth touched his hatbrim to her as she stood beside her husband, her hand resting on his shoulder.

"Why are you here, Elder Booth?" she asked. "If you've thrown in with Dalton Cross, you're no friend of the Lazy S."

"I'm here because of that threat to cut off the water supply conveyed by your man Long. You must know how I would react. If you do anything to disrupt the flow of water to our valley, it will mean disaster for Little Eden. I can't allow that to happen."

"Then leave us alone. Both you and your friend, Cross."

"No. It is not that simple. I have come here to give you and Bill fair warning. Sell out to me or be driven out."

"How much you offering?" Bill asked.

"Two thousand."

"You must be crazy," said Sally.

"In gold."

"We're not selling, Booth," she said.

"Now, wait a minute, Sally," said Bill. He looked at Booth. "You sure you won't go any higher?"

"Maybe I can talk Cross into throwing in another thousand."

"And then you and Cross will get to share the water," Sally broke in. "Is that it?"

"That's what we've agreed to, yes."

"Sally, maybe we should think it over," Bill said.

"No." She looked at Booth, her eyes flashing angrily. "You're a fool, Booth," she told him icily. "Cross wants your valley, too. How long do you think he'll be willing to share that water with you? Think how easy it will be for him to cut you off."

"That's my concern," said Booth. "Will you sell out?"

"No," Sally replied before Bill could speak up.

"Then I'll give you two days to clear out. After that I will not be responsible."

Bill laughed bitterly. "You mean after that you'll let Cross and his hired guns finish what they started."

Booth shrugged. "It is your choice to make."

"Get off my land, Booth," Bill ordered.

"Yes. Go, Elder," added Sally. "You're no longer welcome."

Elder Booth touched his hatbrim to Sally, turned, and strode back to his horse. As he stepped into the saddle, he looked for a long moment back at Bill and Sally. "You're stubborn fools," he pronounced solemnly. "Both of you."

He pulled his horse around and led his riders back out through the gate.

Longarm rode up with Abe and Harry, then dismounted to hear what Booth had wanted. When he was told, Longarm shook his head. "I don't like it."

"What do you mean?" Bill replied. "We stood up to the bastard."

"I got the feeling he didn't come here just to make that offer. It was small enough for him to know you'd never take it—not unless you damn well had to."

"Then why *did* he come here?" Sally asked.

"To check us out, look us over—before making his own move."

"What's he up to, then?" she asked.

"I wish I knew."

The sound of hoofbeats came then, someone riding hard. They turned and saw Diego, astride a nearly spent horse, break over the ridge as he headed toward the compound. The instant Longarm saw how he was slumped over his pommel, he realized Diego was wounded. Without having to be told, Harry and Abe turned their mounts and spurred to meet Diego. They got to him just in time to prevent the Basque from pitching forward off his horse.

A moment later, as Harry and Abe let Diego down on Bill's bed, the Basque looked miserably up at Longarm. "Cross's men took the dam," he gasped. "I couldn't hold it."

"You weren't supposed to," said Longarm. "You were only supposed to keep a lookout."

Sally pushed past Longarm to inspect Diego's wounds. He had been shot twice, in the leg and right arm. Though he had lost considerable blood, both wounds were flesh wounds and reasonably clean. She proceeded to wash and bandage them.

"They came this morning, first thing," Diego told them as Sally worked on him. "Sledge was the Cross D rider in command. I winged a couple of them, maybe—but they come at me from behind. I was lucky to get away."

"Yes, you were," said Sally, finishing up the last bandage. "You shouldn't have tried to fight them."

"What we do now?" Diego asked. "We have no water if Cross say so."

"They won't stop the flow," Longarm assured him. "You'll still have plenty of water for your sheep."

"What about us?" demanded Bill from the doorway where Sally had wheeled him. "The Lazy S won't be able to use that valley any more, or the north range. Cross can stop the flow into that graze any time he wants. With control of that dam, we're at his mercy. Maybe I should've taken Booth's offer."

"I don't think that offer from Booth was on the level, Bill," said Longarm.

"Why in hell not?"

"I figure Booth was here just to keep an eye on us while Cross made his move."

Bill swore angrily.

"But this isn't legal," said Sally. "They've taken our range. Longarm, isn't there anything you can do?"

"I'm not here as a lawman, Sally. Besides, this is not a federal matter. It is a local matter. And there's no law in

Ruby County that I've heard about."

"There's no law," Diego agreed grimly. "I know."

"If there were any," said Bill, "that bastard Booth wouldn't be allowed to run that feudal kingdom of his, complete with harem."

"But now they've made the first move," Longarm went on, "whatever we do now will not be looked at all that closely. And if push comes to shove, I'm sure Marshal Vail will be in our corner."

"So we can move on them?" asked Abe.

"We can move on them."

"When?"

"Now."

"What're we gonna do?"

"I told them what they could expect if they moved against us. Now it's time to make good on that promise. That means I've got a long ride ahead of me—all the way to Ely City."

"Ely City?"

Longarm nodded. "That's a town should have plenty of dynamite on sale."

Abe grinned suddenly. "Hot damn! Now you're talkin'!"

"Abe," Bill said. "What about that rig you said you was fixin' for me so I could ride?"

Abe had selected one of the best leather workers among the Basques to construct, on Longarm's suggestion, a rig that Abe had designed. Fastened to the stirrups, it would enable Bill to sit a horse. "Miguel says it'll be ready in another day or so."

Bill looked at Longarm. "How long will it take for you to get back from Ely City?"

"If I push it, I could be back in two days."

"Then push it."

"Sure, Bill. And while I'm gone, keep a sharp eye out. No telling which way them two snakes're gonna strike now."

Bill fixed Longarm with a cold stare. "You don't have to tell me how to run my end of this, Longarm. But maybe I have to remind you of something." He indicated Sally with a toss of his head. "This here woman behind me is my wife. We got that settled a little while ago."

Longarm smiled easily. "No need to tell me that," Longarm assured him. "I knew it all along."

Despite the unsavory implications of Bill's remark, Longarm was glad to see his old friend so feisty once again. His color had returned somewhat, and he no longer appeared so gaunt, though his eyes still held a bitter light whenever he contemplated his missing legs.

Sally, her face flushed crimson, turned quickly and left the room. In a moment they could hear her fixing coffee. She made a considerable racket while doing so. Bill, turning in his chair to peer into the kitchen, had a grim, malicious smile on his face.

Harry, standing on the other side of the bed alongside Abe, cleared his throat nervously. "I'll be ridin' with you, Longarm."

"Thanks, Harry."

Diego sat up. "I will go now and get my people," he said.

"Stay put," Longarm told him. "No need for that right now. Don't forget, you just lost a lot of blood."

"Diego say he can ride now."

Suiting action to words, the tough little Basque swung his feet off the bed and stood up. He looked blankly around at them for a moment, then promptly collapsed back on the bed, unconscious. Smiling, Longarm lifted the man's legs and set them back onto the bed, then drew a blanket up over the little man.

Glancing across at Harry, Longarm indicated with a quick movement of his head that it was time for them to ride.

They were out of sight of the Lazy S when hoofbeats coming after them caused both men to haul in on their reins and look back. It was Sally.

Harry looked nervously at Longarm. "Want me to keep riding?"

"Might be a good idea at that. I'll catch up."

Harry spurred his mount and Longarm turned his around to wait for Sally. Her face was drawn, her eyes angry sparks when she pulled her mount to a halt alongside Longarm.

"Longarm, I told him."

"Made a clean breast of it, did you?"

"Yes, and I told him why, how I felt . . . about him, his drinking, about us, too."

"That wasn't such a good idea, Sally."

"I don't care. I wanted him to know. Longarm, when this is over, I want to go back to Denver with you."

"That ain't pretty. You leaving a man that's been crippled up."

"He's gone mean. Ain't you seen that? I'd rather have him on the bottle than like this."

"We can't discuss this now."

"I've got to know. Will you take me?"

"You're still his wife, Sally. And right now he needs you. Go on back to him. We'll discuss this later."

She looked full at him then, studying him closely, and he saw in her eyes almost the same level of anger he had read in Bill's. As Longarm started to pull his horse around, her face melted.

"Longarm! Ain't you even goin' to kiss me?"

"Go on back to your husband, Sally. I got some hard riding ahead of me—and you got some thinking to do."

He wheeled his horse and rode after Harry.

Chapter 9

When Longarm and Harry rode into Ely City, it was too late to purchase explosives, but not too late to buy anything—or anyone—else. The booming mining town was going full blast, its bright new street lights illuminating scenes best left in darkness as miners and ladies of the night, in various stages of inebriation and undress, staggered in and out of the town's cribs, saloons, and gambling houses.

Leaving their mounts at the livery, the two men ate a delayed supper at a garish, overpriced restaurant that featured clean tablecloths and real silverware. Then they took a room at a hotel across the street, and afterwards, sighting a barbershop wide open at this late hour, they both got baths, haircuts, and shaves. Feeling prosperous and a mite lucky, Harry left Longarm to try his luck at the tables of the Gold Nugget, a gambling parlor and saloon next door to the hotel.

Longarm had a few drinks in as quiet a saloon as he could find, then went back to the hotel alone. He was starting up the second flight of stairs when a shadow materialized behind him. He heard just enough to cause him to crouch low and spin, his Colt materializing in his right hand. Kristen jumped back, staring wide-eyed into the .44's yawning bore.

"Kristen! What in hell are you doing, coming up on me like that?" Longarm demanded. "You're lucky I didn't blow your head off."

"Please, Custis," she said, "put away that gun. I'm sorry

I startled you. But I had to see you."

Longarm holstered his Colt and straightened up, taking a deep breath to give his nerves a chance to stop jangling. "Hell, Kristen. You know that's no problem," he told her. "I'll be glad to see you any time. You got any objection to my room?"

"Of course not."

He took her by the arm and guided her up the stairs ahead of him, unlocked the door to his room, and followed in after her. Then he closed the door behind him and locked it.

She looked past him at the locked door. "Did you have to do that?"

"Just didn't want to be disturbed."

She nodded and slumped wearily back onto the bed, her hands clasped in her lap. "It's that damn elder," she said. "I knew he wouldn't leave me be."

He smiled. "Out with it, Kristen. What's he up to now?"

Taking him by the arm, Kristen drew him over to the window. Pulling the curtains back just enough for them to see an alley across the street, she indicated with a nod of her head two men standing in its shadows. They were hulking men, dressed in Mormon black, and those passing the alley mouth gave them a wide berth.

"Those two men. See them?" she asked.

Longarm nodded. "I see them."

"They're after me. They've come to bring me back."

"To Elder Booth?"

"Yes. He's the one sent them."

"They look like Destroying Angels."

"They are."

Kristen stepped back from the window. Longarm walked with her over to the bed. The room was still in darkness and Longarm did not make any effort to light a lamp.

"Let's have it," Longarm told her, as he sat down on the edge of the bed beside her.

"When I first got back, I worked in Millie's parlor house,"

106

Kristen said, "and things were goin' well enough, but after a couple of days Millie told me she would have to let me go. She said she had some new girls comin' in and didn't have room for me."

"You believe that?"

"I didn't have any choice. Anyway, I didn't let that bother me. I went into the Silver Slipper and worked at their faro and blackjack tables for a couple of nights. I did the place some good, Longarm. But Sam Feeley, the owner, told me he had to let me go."

"Did he tell you why?"

"He did. He . . . owed me a favor, you might say, so he told me what he could. He said Elder Booth had sent two men into Ely City to get me. He said Booth was mean enough to send the rest of his night riders in if he wanted to—and there'd be no one to stop him. Those two across the street, Custis, they are the ones Booth sent."

"When did you learn all this?"

"This afternoon."

"So you've been keeping away from them."

She nodded forlornly. "I been keeping to crowded places, so if they tried to grab me, there'd be witnesses. But they almost got me an hour ago when I was passing an alley farther down. You can't believe how glad I was to see you ride in."

"And you've been waiting on those stairs for me since."

"The desk clerk gave me your room number."

"What about that gent you was all set to nail to the wall, the gambler who sold you to Booth in the first place."

"He's gone. Lit out. No one knows where he is."

"So it's just them two down there now we got to worry about."

"Yes."

"They must've seen you duck in here."

"I . . . think they did, Custis."

"And they couldn't have missed me coming in just now. They won't have any trouble putting two and two together."

107

"I had no choice, Custis. I had to come here. I had nowhere else to go."

Longarm got up and went back to the window. The two night riders were still down there, still smoking, waiting for Kristen to leave so they could make their move and ride out with their prize through silent streets. But they'd be wary now they knew she was up here with Longarm.

Still at the window, he turned to look at Kristen sitting on the bed. "As long as they're in that alley, we're safe," he told her. Then he grinned. "I suppose you ought to be complimented. The elder's going to a lot of trouble to get you back."

"I'd rather die first."

"You won't have to—and that's a promise."

She sighed in relief, then tipped her head quizzically. "Mr. Long, what are you doing in Ely City?"

He told her enough to satisfy her. She leaned back on the bed. "I don't care about all that land-grabbing and talk about water rights. All I want is to be free of that bastard."

He left the window and stood over her. She looked up at him and smiled. In the moonlight coming through the window, her pale face had a soft, childlike glow to it, and her long pale hair flowed over the bedspread like molten silver. Abruptly, she opened her arms to him.

"We haven't been together in a long time, Mr. Long," she reminded him, her voice suddenly husky. "The hell with those bastards out there."

"If you hadn't said that, I would've," he admitted as he sat down beside her on the bed, thrust his Colt under the pillow, and began to pull off his boots. "By the way," he said as he kicked away the boots. "My friends call me Longarm."

"Mmmm," she murmured afterward, her arms still around his neck, her body splayed loosely under him. "You are wonderful."

"Let me check if them two are still down there," he said.

He padded over to the window and, pushing aside the curtains, saw them still standing there. It didn't look as if they had moved an inch. He moved back to the bed and flopped down beside Kristen.

"They haven't moved."

"You see? When you're with me, time stands still," she chuckled.

"Is that it?"

"What shall we do now?"

"What we just been doin' would suit me fine," he drawled, feasting his eyes on her rounded hips and full belly. Reaching over, he placed a hand on one of her breasts, flicked his big thumb over her pink nipple, and felt it spring to life under his ministrations.

Laughing, she reached down and fondled him. "Mmm," she said, laughing huskily, "I see you ain't spent yet."

"Try me."

Laughing, her teeth found his hairy chest and she burrowed into him like something wild. He didn't know who came first or which one stopped first and he didn't care as they clung together fiercely. After a long, delicious interval, he collapsed beside her on the bed, panting. He heard her soft, low chuckle of satisfaction, then felt her lips caressing his sweaty forehead.

"Don't let me sleep long," he told her. "And keep an eye on those two downstairs."

She murmured assent and kissed his forehead lightly. He closed his eyes and slept.

Kristen was leaning close over him, the nipples of her breasts brushing the hair on his chest.

"Longarm!" she whispered, her voice betraying her fear. "They're not down there in the alley. They're gone!"

Awake instantly, Longarm swung off the bed and reached for his Colt under the pillow. As he pulled it out, Kristen darted to a far corner. At that moment the door was flung open and the two men from the alley burst in.

Longarm slammed to the floor as both men cut loose with their sixguns. The powerful detonations caused the room's walls to reverberate powerfully. Hot lead slammed into the bed, sending a storm of feathers into the air. A bullet clattered through the bedsprings and struck the back of Longarm's leg, searing it, before rolling onto the floor.

The two men paused to peer through the gunsmoke at the bed. Longarm fired up twice at the foremost gunman and saw the man buck and fold, then slump head down to the floor. His companion, closer to the door, sent a wild shot in Longarm's direction and vanished into the hallway. Scrambling to his feet, Longarm leaped over the bullet-riddled gunslick on the floor and cut down the hallway just in time to catch sight of the back of his would-be assailant's head as he plunged frantically down the stairs.

In the lobby at the foot of the stairs, the fleeing man turned and fired up at Longarm. Ducking, Longarm squinted through the wood splinters plowed up by the bullet and saw the gray, pocked face of his old friend, Sam Connell. Seeing he had missed, Connell turned and ran across the lobby and out the door, with Longarm, stark naked, close behind him. Connell headed for the alley across the street and reached it before Longarm could overtake him.

Behind him, Longarm heard outraged women screaming and men crying out for the town marshal. Paying no heed, he plunged into the alley after Connell. Close to its end, the blackness ahead of him exploded into light, and death whispered past his ear. Crouching swiftly, he sent two, then three quick shots at the spot just below the flash. He didn't stop until his hammer came down on an empty chamber.

When the echo of the rapid detonations faded, Longarm heard the sound of a man thrashing on the ground before him—thrashing and cursing. Longarm moved forward cautiously, aware that a wounded man with a gun in his hand was still dangerous. When he got close enough to see the man clearly, he kicked Connell's gun away and gazed down at the man Booth referred to as a cockroach. Connell was

110

still alive, but just barely. He was sprawled in the mud of the alley, his life's blood draining away from a bullet wound in his thigh, another in his neck, and a third just above his belt buckle.

As the alley filled with townsmen, a barkeep brushed past Longarm and held a lantern over Connell. Slowly, convulsively, like a stomped worm, the dying man twisted on the ground, blood bubbling from his mouth. A few women turned abruptly and went skittering away, heads down, while still more citizens poured into the alley, creating a solid circle of staring faces.

As men with lanterns burst through the spectators, someone flung a frock coat over Longarm's shoulders.

Longarm turned. It was Harry.

"Hell of a way to conduct yourself," Harry told him. "Running around with no clothes on, gunning down innocent citizens."

"He wasn't innocent. He tried to kill me."

"Who is he?"

"Sam Connell. He's the one trailed us out of Ruby. Used to work for Cross until he switched sides and went to work for Booth."

The town marshal and two deputies arrived and pushed their way through the crowd to examine Connell. Longarm stepped back while the marshal bent to listen for a heartbeat. After a moment he shook his head and stood up. Scanning the crowd, he caught sight of the oddly-dressed Longarm—and the Colt in his hand.

"What in hell's goin' on here?" he demanded.

"It was self-defense, Marshal," Longarm replied.

The marshal, a tall man with a handlebar mustache and a gleaming star pinned to his vest, walked closer and studied Longarm. Longarm realized the man was wondering if this wasn't some kind of fool practical joke—that maybe the man on the ground ought to jump up any minute now and cry, "Surprise!"

"I guess maybe you're wondering what I'm doing traipsing around town in this uniform," Longarm suggested.

"That's right," replied the town marshal. "I sure as hell am."

"I left my room in a hurry. I was chasing this one."

"But you say you shot this man in self-defense?"

Longarm nodded. "He'd been shooting at me since he broke into my room at the hotel."

"I see," the town marshal said, looking back down uncertainly at the sprawled, bloody body.

"That man I shot calls himself Sam Connell," Longarm continued. "He had an accomplice. I shot him, too."

"You did, did you?"

Longarm nodded.

"And where's he?"

"Upstairs in my room. Or he was last time I saw him."

The town marshal sighed wearily. "Guess maybe you'd better take me up there."

With Harry at his side, Longarm pushed his way through the crowd and started across the street to the hotel. After directing his deputies to get help for the dying man, the wary town marshal followed after them.

When Longarm reached his floor, he found the hallway outside his door packed almost solid with hotel guests. The bellhops were having some difficulty keeping them back. Pushing through the crowd, Longarm entered the room. Kristen was gone, but not the body of the man he had shot. He was still lying face down on the floor, a dark puddle of blood congealing on the wooden floor under his chest.

Harry dropped beside the intruder and, turning him over, pressed the back of his hand against the man's cheek, then looked up at Longarm and shook his head.

Longarm turned to the marshal. "This was the first one broke into my room. The other one bolted back down the stairs when I opened up."

The marshal's eyebrows went up a notch. "I recognize this one," he said. "I don't know that one out in the alley, but this one's a Mormon working for the elder. A mean

112

bastard, he was." He looked at Longarm. "Word in town was this man was after a woman—him and his sidekick."

"Kristen."

"Yeah. That's the one."

Longarm shrugged. "Maybe they were and changed their minds. The elder and me ain't exactly on the best of terms."

"That don't bother me none," the town marshal said, smiling suddenly. "From what I heard, this bastard here had it comin' to him. Meanwhile, take my advice, mister, and get some clothes on. That suit coat don't go down near far enough."

The deputies joined the marshal then and the three took charge, seeing to the removal of the Mormon's body, while the hotel manager was summoned to relocate Longarm and Harry to a less bloody room. Once the manager had done so and Longarm and Harry were alone, Longarm gave Harry a brief rundown of his night's adventures, not leaving out Kristen's visit.

Then, fully dressed, Longarm started from the room.

"Where you goin' now?" Harry asked.

"I got some questions for Kristen—if I can find her. You go on and get some shuteye. I won't be long."

Longarm had no trouble finding Kristen. She was in the back of the crowd, watching Sam Connell's dead body being carried on a makeshift stretcher to the undertaker's.

"Hello, Kristen."

She whirled and stared up at him. "Longarm! You're all right!"

"Nary a scratch."

"I'm so glad!"

He took her none too gently by the arm and steered her toward a small restaurant that was still open. Inside, they found a table in a corner. He ordered coffee for both of them.

"Surprised to see me, weren't you?" he told her.

"Of course I was. I didn't know what happened to you

after you ran out of the room. By the time I got dressed and ran downstairs, there was just that crowd in the alley."

"You didn't see me return to the hotel and go back upstairs? Half this town was watching. You had to see me, unless you ducked out the back way. Did you?"

She hesitated a moment, then nodded. "I was . . . frightened."

"Of who?"

"Of those men."

"Hell, Kristen! Speak the truth, for once. It was me you were afraid of."

"Of you? That's crazy!"

"Is it?"

Their coffee arrived. She pulled hers toward her slowly, watching him warily. "Longarm, what are you getting at?"

"Look, Kristen. The only reason I'm talking to you now is I have to know if those two were the only ones after me."

"After you?"

"You heard me."

"But I told you. It was me they were after!"

He smiled at her. "As soon as they saw Harry and me ride in, they forgot all about you. The elder's price on my head was a lot higher than the one on yours. So Connell and his pal went to you and made a deal."

"Longarm! How can you say that?"

"Why else would you unlock the door to let them in?"

Her face went pale. "But that's not true! I warned you!"

"Yes. And that's what saved my life. I'm grateful, Kristen. So tell me, what went on in that crazy female head of yours? You have a change of heart at the last minute?"

To Longarm's surprise, there were tears running down her cheeks. She nodded. "When I heard their footsteps, I couldn't go through with it. That's why I ran over and woke you up. But it was too late."

"Almost too late. Now, tell me. Were those two men the only night riders Booth sent after you?"

"Yes."

"And that's the truth?"

"So help me God, Longarm."

Longarm leaned back and sipped his coffee, studying Kristen's lovely face. God help him, but she *was* beautiful.

"Will you ever forgive me, Longarm?"

Longarm pondered her question. He supposed he didn't blame her for letting those two have a go at him. Whichever way it went, it was the smart play for her. Whether Longarm killed those two night riders or they killed him, either way she got her freedom—at least temporarily.

"Don't let it bother you," he told her. "I don't hold grudges."

She caught the chill in his voice. Peering closely across the table at him, she wiped her eyes with a corner of a napkin. "But—between us—it will never be the same, will it?"

It was a great show, the way she could turn the water-works on and off like that. She must have had a switch somewhere. He didn't feel it would be proper to remind her that there hadn't been all that much between them to begin with, so he just nodded. "Guess not," he said.

"Well, anyway," she replied, tossing her head defiantly, "them two bastards are dead—and you aren't. That's something."

She got up without finishing her coffee and bent swiftly to kiss him on the forehead. Then, with a wave, she strolled from the restaurant. He watched the door close behind her, then finished his coffee and headed back to his hotel.

He had a long ride ahead of him tomorrow, and he needed his sleep—or what sleep he could still manage after this crazy night.

Chapter 10

To Longarm and Harry's astonishment, Bill rode out to greet them as they entered Lazy S range. He rode stiffly, bent a little forward over the pommel, his face compressed grimly as he fought back the pain; but he impressed both men as he pulled his mount around and continued to ride alongside them.

"The rig's workin' out fine," Harry said to Bill.

"It'll do," Bill replied.

"Looks like it hurts some," Longarm commented.

"I'll get used to it. At least I'm out of that goddamned chair. That the dynamite, in them boxes?"

Bill was referring to the four boxes, two each strapped onto their pommels. Longarm nodded.

"No trouble getting it?"

"Longarm had a little trouble with one of them Destroying Angels," Harry told Bill, "him and his sidekick. When it was done, it was them was destroyed. The next morning the store owner was so happy to get them two no-accounts off the street, he let us have the dynamite for cost and gave us an extra box of fuses."

Bill looked at Longarm. "You say you took out two of Booth's night riders?"

Longarm nodded.

"Good. That's two less we got to worry about."

Longarm said nothing.

"What's next?" Bill asked.

"We blow the dam."

"When?"

"Tonight."

"Who's we?"

"Harry and me," Longarm told him.

"I can ride now. What about me?"

"We'll be afoot, mostly—ducking down the side of that canyon, planting the stuff, and keeping clear of Cross's men at the same time. Be better anyway if you, Abe, and Diego stay back to guard the ranch."

Bill thought that over, then shrugged. "All right," he said grudgingly.

They were in sight of the Lazy S ranch house by this time. Longarm was surprised to see how much work the Basques had completed on the two barns. The knock of hammers and the steady rasp of saws cutting through fresh wood echoed sharply across the flat.

When they pulled up in the front yard, Diego and Abe stepped out of a barn and waved. Longarm and Harry waved back as Bill spurred suddenly on ahead of them toward the cottonwood. Pulling up alongside his wheelchair, he reached up and grabbed two ropes hanging from a limb and lifted himself deftly out of his saddle rig. A cluck to the horse caused it to turn away and walk out from under the tree while Bill lowered himself deftly into his wheelchair. He was smugly proud of his accomplishment as he looked up at Longarm and Harry, who were pulling to a halt beside him.

"See that?" he said. "And I can get on just as easily."

Longarm was thinking that if Bill rode very far, such as into town or out on the range to check on his stock, he would find it considerably awkward lugging that cottonwood tree around with him. But he said nothing to discourage Bill.

"Can't keep a good man down," said Harry approvingly.

Longarm and Harry dismounted. Sally came out of the

118

ranch house to greet them. Her face showed little emotion, and she did not look directly at Longarm as she spoke. "You're just in time for supper," she said. "Wash up. It's on the table."

"Yes, ma'am!" said Harry, pleased.

"We'll be right in," Longarm replied.

She nodded curtly to Longarm, a sad, fleeting smile lighting her face, then took hold of the back of Bill's wheelchair and pushed him up onto the low porch, using a ramp Abe had constructed. Taking Bill's horse along with his own, Longarm strode toward the nearly completed barn with Harry.

The two men walked in silence, Longarm absorbed in his own troubled thoughts. Things were not good between Bill and Sally, and Longarm knew he had to accept some of the blame. But what angered him most was that, as she had admitted to him earlier, she had told everything to Bill. There had been no damn need for that. Longarm had always wondered at the perverse streak in some women who found such pleasure in making sure their husbands found out. Part of the joy in their infidelity, he had long realized, was the joy they took in personally pinning the horns on the cuckold.

The table was crowded, with Diego and four of his men joining the rest of them, but Sally fed them all. At the meal's conclusion, with the table cleared off except for the coffee and fresh doughnuts Sally put down for them, Longarm outlined his plan. He and Harry would blow the dam that night. The next day or later, he assumed, the elder's men, along with a force sent by Cross, possibly, would storm the canyon in order to repair the dam. But by then the Lazy S would have dug in and would have little trouble defending their ground.

"Meanwhile," Longarm finished up, "I figure Cross is going to take another swipe at the Lazy S, so the rest of you stay close to the ranch and keep your eyes peeled for trouble."

Diego's round, nut-brown face smiled in appreciation of Longarm's plan. He looked at Longarm, chuckling. "Booth will not like it, to see his irrigation ditches dry up like that. Maybe then his women can go inside in the shade and sit down for while, maybe."

"Without water," Bill asked, "how long do you think it'll be before Booth cries uncle?"

"In this high sun, I figure his fields shouldn't last more'n a week without water—maybe not even that long."

Diego and his men exchanged pleased glances, their dark eyes gleaming at the thought of Elder Booth's crops yellowing under the hot sun.

Sally looked nervously around the table. "My god. This sounds exactly like a war."

"It's close to it," acknowledged Longarm. "But all you'll be doing is defending your land and your property. The moment Cross moved onto Lazy S land to take that dam, the law was on our side."

"It's on our side if we survive," Bill said. "Otherwise, it won't matter one way or the other."

"Bill," Longarm said, "let's get this clear from the first. If you and Sally want to move out right now, I'm sure Cross or the elder would not raise a hand to stop you. Hell, maybe the elder would still pay you what he offered."

"No." Bill spat bitterly. "I'm sorry I even considered it for a moment. No one is taking our land without a fight!"

"I feel the same way," said Sally.

Longarm glanced across the table at Harry. "Let's get going," he told him. "I figure tonight's a fine night for fireworks."

They were crossing a moonlit patch of grass a couple of hours later when a rider nudged his horse out of cover just ahead of them, his rifle barrel gleaming as it rested across his pommel. One look at the slight, gray figure and both men knew at once who it was.

"Abe!" Longarm cried. "What in blazes are you doing out here?"

"Thought I'd tag along," he said, putting his horse down the slope toward them. "I think maybe you two need me more'n you might think."

"How's that?" Harry asked, as Abe pulled alongside.

"I know that canyon—and a way to get close, real close to the dam without showing yourself. For one thing, the way you're goin' now, you'll have to cross open ground before reaching it."

"If you know a better way, lead on," Longarm told him.

Abe nodded decisively. "Follow me."

At once they turned off the trail they were following and began a steep climb into the peaks north of them. Just past midnight they tethered their horses in a grassy spot. Then, each one lugging a box of explosives, they picked their way down through a cleft in the canyon wall and came out almost immediately on a ledge not a hundred feet above the dam. Carefully putting down the explosives, they moved to the edge and gazed down at the dam and the still, black waters backed up behind it.

"Over there," Abe said quietly, pointing.

They looked and saw, less than half a mile below the dam, two smouldering campfires alongside the stream, glowing in the darkness of the flat like a pair of cat's eyes.

"We blow this dam, them fellers down there're goin' to have to move—and move fast," Harry commented wryly.

"There must be others up here in the rocks," Longarm noted. "We'd better look around and clean them out quietly."

"While we're at it," Abe said, pointing to a faint glow on the other side of the canyon that seemed to be coming from a nest of boulders close by the dam, "maybe we better check that out, too."

"It's too steady for a campfire," said Harry.

"More like a lantern," Abe agreed.

"Abe," Longarm said, "you work your way down this

side and see what you can find. Harry and I'll cross over on the dam and see who's crowdin' that lantern or whatever it is."

Without argument, Abe let himself over the edge and disappeared into the darkness. Longarm and Harry followed. Once they reached the dam, they crossed it on a shaky log catwalk, then jumped across the spillway into darkness and came down onto a rocky trail, the glow they were following visible just beyond a clump of rocks. Reaching them, they paused to listen and heard the low murmur of voices and an occasional bark of mean laughter.

Longarm and Harry kept on around the rocks and saw just ahead of them three men kneeling on a slicker playing poker, a lantern sitting beside them. Longarm pointed to the nearest one and then to Harry. Harry nodded. Longarm then pointed to the one beside Harry's man and back to himself, then indicated the fellow on the far side of the lantern, this time pointing to himself and Harry. Harry grinned and moved out toward the poker players, his gun held out before him like a club.

A split second later Harry crashed the barrel of his Colt down onto his man's skull, while Longarm slammed his own victim into the darkness with one swipe of his gun barrel. Without pause, he launched himself at the third poker player. As the man went down under him, Longarm glimpsed a pair of wide, startled eyes and a mouth gaping open to cry out.

Longarm clapped his hand over the man's mouth. The fellow bit him. Yanking his hand back, Longarm doubled up his fist and punched him on the point of his jaw. The poker player's head snapped around and Longarm heard his jawbone crack. Uttering a muffled, constricted cry, the man grabbed at his face. By that time Harry had joined Longarm, cracking the fellow on the side of his noggin with the barrel of his .44.

The third poker player flopped over and lay still.

Longarm and Harry looked around. Three unconscious

men were lying on their backs, the lantern, untouched in the brief struggle, sending a soft glow over their slack faces. The two men left the lantern burning and hurried back across the dam, clambering back up to where they had left their explosives. Abe was already waiting for them.

"Find anyone?" he asked Abe.

"I found one," Abe told him, just as quietly. "But he didn't see me until it was too late. He'll be asleep for a while."

"Only one?"

"That's all I could find."

Longarm glanced warily about him at the dark walls of the canyon. He couldn't help but feel that there were others they had not yet discovered still planted about them in the rocks.

"Well, let's get these charges set," Longarm said, opening one of the boxes of explosives.

A moment later, three makeshift charges strapped to his back, Longarm led the way back down the slope, heading this time for the canyon floor in front of the dam. As he picked his way carefully down the steep slope, he realized somewhat ruefully that the three of them were now little more than walking bombs. A single shot out of the blackness surrounding them could instantly ignite the dynamite strapped to them, sending into the night sky and across the black slopes, chunks of bloody bone and gristle for the buzzards to feed on come daylight.

Longarm forced himself not to think of this and concentrated instead on the business at hand. Before leaving the Lazy S, Harry and he had fashioned charges out of six sticks of dynamite tied together with bailing wire, with blasting caps tamped in carefully. Attaching the Bickford fuses, they cut them to a length calculated to insure detonation approximately four minutes after being lit. Taking advantage of Abe's unexpected arrival, Longarm had decided to set a third charge in the center of the dam, with the other two at each end. To himself he had assigned the farthest charge,

123

with Harry set to plant the middle charge, and Abe the one closest to the trail leading back up to the ledge.

Reaching the canyon floor, Longarm paused to glance up at the dam, a crude but efficient breastwork of logs braced solidly against the sheer canyon walls on either side. Packed in solidly between the logs was a mixture of mud and brush and clay that had hardened by this time almost to the consistency of cement. Though a crude, not very professional-looking structure, in the darkness the dam looked formidable enough, and Longarm now wondered if their three charges would be sufficient to breach it.

A glance behind him showed Harry moving along. He kept going, the talus moving treacherously under his feet. He slipped more than once in the darkness, but each time managed to reach out to the dam's log wall for support. Reaching the far end of the dam under the spillway, Longarm used the butt of his .44 to help claw the mud out from between the logs.

Once his charges were planted firmly, he looked back and saw first one, then another handkerchief waving dimly in the moonlit, the signal that Harry and Abe had finished planting their charges as well. The plan agreed upon beforehand was that Longarm would light his fuse with a gunshot, then signal for them to do the same. The three shots, Longarm figured, would give some warning at least to Cross's men camped on the flat below the dam.

Taking out his Colt, Longarm straightened the end of the fuse to give himself a better target, then fired. The fuse began sputtering. As he raced back along the base of the dam, two more shots rang out almost simultaneously as Abe and Harry lit their own fuses. Running hard now, Longarm saw Abe and Harry already clambering up the steep slope.

Reaching the slope seconds after them, Longarm pulled himself rapidly up toward the ledge. He was almost to it when Harry reached down to help him scramble up the few remaining feet. Just as he gained the ledge, Longarm heard a rifle's sharp crack. Clutching at his thigh, Harry groaned and sagged forward onto the ground. Longarm glanced up to see a rifleman standing on a rock about fifty feet above them, his frame outlined clearly against the moonlit sky. Instantly, Abe and Longarm opened up. The rifleman vanished from sight, uttering a sharp cry that ceased abruptly. At once more gunfire erupted from the darkness around them.

Longarm ducked low as the whining bullets ricocheted about him. As he had suspected all along, they had been working inside a beehive and had been lucky enough not to alert a single bee—until now.

Crawling over to Harry, Longarm helped the man crawl into the protection of some rocks as the rifle fire and gunfire continued pouring out of the darkness around them. Aiming at the flashes, he and Abe did their best to return the fire, but it was obvious they were only wasting ammunition.

"We can't stay here," Longarm told Abe.

"Hell, I know that!"

"Harry, can you keep up?" Longarm asked him.

"Sure. Let's go."

But as soon as Harry took more than a couple of steps, he stumbled and went down, twisting in pain.

"Where are you hit?" Longarm asked him.

"The right leg," Harry muttered weakly. "You two better leave me here. Save yourselves."

"Not bloody likely," said Longarm, and slung Harry over his shoulder.

With Abe leading the way, they ducked back up through the cleft in the rocks. A moment later reached their horses. The first blast came. A second later, the rest of the dynamite detonated, the series of titanic concussions shaking the ground enough to hurl both Longarm and Harry forward. Abe helped them to their feet, then helped Harry up onto Longarm's horse, with Longarm climbing up behind the wounded man and holding him upright.

As they rode free of the rocks, they pulled to a halt on a patch of high ground to watch what was happening below

125

them. In the pale flood of the moon's light, they saw what appeared to be a vast cauldron of boiling water surging across the flat. At the crest of the flood were the logs that had formed the dam's breastwork, together with trees and boulders and what appeared to be great chunks of earth. With these as a battering ram, the wall of water was sweeping everything before it, undercutting ridges and hillocks as it surged across the flat. It was this sudden devastating flood of water that was causing the ground under them to tremble. To Longarm it seemed as if the air itself was trembling, with a muttering, buffeting force that beat on them like a sullen wind.

"Jesus," said Abe, his voice reflecting the awe he felt at this example of the water's unleashed power.

"Yeah," agreed Longarm.

Longarm could see no trace of Cross's men struggling in the water, but it did not seem likely that many had escaped, despite the last-minute warning Longarm had contrived for them.

As the three men watched, the swift, dark tide of water dropped beyond the flat and disappeared into the hills below. There were no settlements that Longarm was aware of in the flood path, and by dawn the water would have gouged out a new channel before it dissipated finally in the lower valleys and canyons. He had no doubt the original river channel was now completely obliterated. It was doubtful if this stream would ever find again the channel it had followed for so many ages.

"You all right, Harry?" Longarm asked.

"Let's get the hell out of here," Harry said. "I'm losing blood and it hurts like a son of a bitch."

Longarm and Abe pulled their horses around and spurred on through the night, the sound of the roaring water fading slowly behind them.

Chapter 11

Two days later, looking down at the wreckage of the dam and the broad, muddy gash in the flat left by the sudden torrent of water, Longarm saw for the first time in broad daylight the devastation caused by the dam's destruction. The stream leaving the canyon had already carved out a new channel for itself, but as Longarm had expected, it was not the same channel. The stream appeared to have shifted almost a quarter of a mile to the east by the time it vanished below the flat.

Bill and Diego were with him. Harry was back at the Lazy S with Abe. It was Abe who had taken the bullet out of Harry's thigh and Sally who now kept the bandages fresh. The barn had been completed by Diego and his men, and Bill, sullenly insistent on showing them how adept he had become at handling a mount in his special rig, had joined Longarm and Diego in this inspection of the dam site. Though Cross's men had abandoned it, Longarm was sure the elder would have to send men out to take the site back and rebuild the dam. He had no alternative. It was either that or the finish of Little Eden.

The rest of the Basques in the region had rallied around the Lazy S by this time, and with Diego as their leader, they were prepared to defend the canyon and keep Booth from going to the canyon site to rebuild the dam. Already Diego's men had selected their positions high in the rocks above the canyon's entrance.

Longarm asked Diego if all his men had arrived and were in position.

"I'll ride to see Emil," Diego told Longarm. "He is on other side of canyon with his men."

"We'll be here waiting," Longarm said, as he dismounted.

As Diego turned his horse and rode off, Bill nudged his horse closer to the canyon's edge and started down. "Sally and I worked hard to build that dam," he told Longarm wearily. "You can't imagine what it took. First it was luggin' them logs all the way up here, then setting them in so they spanned the canyon floor. It took a whole summer for us to fill in the breastworks with earth; then each year we piled it a few feet higher. Now, after all that, it's gone."

"Why did you bother?"

"It meant we'd always have water. Always."

"When did the elder stick his nose into it?"

"A couple of years after we started the dam. He suggested we build it high enough to spill water out of the other end of the canyon and down the far slope. He had studied the terrain and saw where the water would follow a series of natural channels and gullies until it reached a spot just above Little Eden. He said he could catch it there and shunt it through wooden sluices that would feed directly into his valley's irrigation system. He said it would transform his valley."

"He was right, from what I've seen of it."

"I know."

"Did he help you increase the dam's capacity?"

"Sure. He sent his women over." Bill shook his head. "They lived in tents there on the flat and worked liked coolies, carrying earth in wheelbarrows up planks so steep I didn't dare look."

"He'll be back again before long."

"But not with his women this time. I don't care. I say, let 'em come. He was always telling me he could have built

128

a better, more efficient dam. Well, now we'll see about that."

Two days later Elder Booth made his move.

Alerted to the advance of Elder Booth's forces by Diego's men, Bill and Longarm, with a sizable number of sheepherders brandishing everything from flintlocks to Winchesters, took positions above the dam site and watched as the Mormons approached, a line of covered wagons in the center, an escort of mounted riders on each side.

Bill remained on his horse behind Longarm, who had tethered his horse and was now sprawled alongside Diego. From his height it was Bill who first caught sight of the women.

"Those ain't men in them wagons," he called down to Longarm. "Just like before, I'm thinking—and each one of them with a pick or a shovel."

Longarm glanced at Diego. "Tell your men not to fire until I fire first, and not to fire at the wagons, only the men mounted alongside the wagons."

Diego scrambled to his feet, mounted up, and trotted off toward the rocks.

"Help me down," said Bill.

"Why?"

"I got my rifle. I can help. But I can't do much strapped up here on top of this horse."

Longarm got up and, after a moment of fiddling with the buckles and straps, lifted Bill down. The man used his elbows to pull himself along the ground with his rifle, taking Diego's position alongside Longarm.

Watching him settle into a good firing position, Longarm asked, "You comfortable enough there?"

"Comfortable? Do you realize how much a man needs his legs to do *anything* comfortable?"

"Never thought of it before."

"Be glad you don't have to."

Longarm looked back down at the approaching Mormons. They were still well out of rifle range, and Longarm was surprised they were approaching the canyon so directly, wondering if this wasn't meant to be some kind of diversion.

"Maybe we should be expecting them to be flanking us," he muttered to Bill, his eyes on the three approaching columns.

"Why should they? The elder's countin' on us being afraid of shootin' at his women. He knows what kind of a stink that would create in these parts."

Longarm frowned. Bill was right. That was what the elder was counting on—the Lazy S's unwillingness to slaughter defenseless women, even if they were rebuilding the dam.

Each wagon could be seen quite clearly now, along with the bonneted woman driving the teams. And then Longarm was able to point out to Bill the long-skirted women plodding along beside the wagons. Bill began to chuckle meanly then as they caught sight of the women riding alongside the wagons. They weren't all women, but a good many of them were.

"Son of a bitch," Longarm muttered. "That bastard ain't so dumb, after all. He's got us boxed in."

"What'd I tell you?" Bill said, taking a whiskey flask from his back pocket. Unscrewing it, he downed at least half of what was in the flask, gulping greedily. Screwing the cap back on, he put the flask back into his pocket and wiped his mouth.

"How about sharing some of that?" Longarm suggested, lighting up a fresh cheroot. He thought he had given up smoking, but this vacation away from Denver had caused him to bury that resolve damn quick.

Bill glanced at him, his eyes gleaming with sudden malevolence. "Why should I share my booze? I've already shared enough with you."

"Why don't you forget about that, Bill?"

"Funny thing. It's like these two stumps I got now instead

130

of legs. I can't forget them either."

"Maybe if you'd stop feeling sorry for yourself and put away the booze, things would go better between you and Sally."

"That your advice, is it?"

"Just trying to help."

"Some help, you are. A real friend."

"Funny thing is, Bill, that's what I am."

"I tell you what. I'd rather you were my enemy, and I still had a wife."

"You still have."

"She's leavin' me. She told me that before I rode out with you and Diego today."

"I'm sorry," Longarm said.

"You goin' to say you didn't know nothin' about that?"

"I didn't say that."

"It don't matter. I'm here to tell you, Longarm. If Sally goes, I'll see to it you two ain't in no condition to meet up later."

Longarm felt an icy finger move up his spine. In Bill's bitter, implacable eyes he read murder, a cold unemotional commitment to sending a bullet into Longarm's—or his wife's—spine. It was a resolve as simple and as terrible as that.

And there was nothing Longarm could do about it.

By this time the wagons and their escort were well within range of Longarm's Winchester, and of the rifles of every other man in Longarm's force. Longarm now saw that the great majority of those riding alongside the wagons were Mormon women. If Longarm's men opened up on the few men mixed in with the women, the resulting slaughter of women caught in the crossfire would be intolerable.

At last, unwilling to be the first to open fire, Longarm stood up in plain view of the Mormons and watched with intense frustration as the wagons disappeared below him into the canyon.

A moment later Diego rode up to rejoin them. As he dismounted, his wizened countenance revealed the same bafflement Longarm felt. "We are fighting Mormon women," he told Longarm. "Already these women of the Mormons take shovel and pick from wagons and begin to dig. Some even have logs in their wagons to fix dam."

Propping his back up against a boulder, Bill looked coldly up at Longarm. "What now?"

Longarm shrugged. "I can't see us killing them. And maybe it wouldn't be such a bad idea to let them rebuild the dam."

"You must be crazy."

"We need the dam—or at least the Lazy S does if it wants to use the north pasture—so why bother them? Meanwhile, I'll go on down there and talk to the Mormon in charge."

"Why?"

"To set up a meeting with the elder."

"What for?"

"To deal."

"What kind of deal?"

"That he dissolve this sudden partnership of his with Cross and help us rebuild the dam, then stay out of any further disputes you have with Cross."

"He'd never do that. What would he get in return?"

"Water. Once his women have rebuilt the dam, all the water he needs to irrigate Little Eden. We guarantee him this as long as he leaves the Lazy S alone."

Bill thought it over, then looked hopefully up at Longarm. "You think he'd go for it?"

"He doesn't have a choice. He knows we can blow up the dam as many times as he can rebuild it. I suspect he's waiting right now to make a deal. He's already learned how much he can rely on the Cross D gunslicks to keep this dam intact."

Bill's face showed sudden resolve. "Do it."

"I will. Diego and I'll help you onto your horse. Ride back to the Lazy S and keep an eye on things. I'm still worried about Cross. You can tell Sally what we're up to, if you want."

"If she cares," Bill said bitterly.

As Longarm and Diego lifted Bill onto his horse a moment later and then helped strap him to the stirrups, Longarm felt just a mite edgy. For his part, Bill submitted to their help with little grace and an awkward silence as the two men's fingers fumbled and caught at the straps and buckles. It was the first design, and Longarm could see it was going to need some improvements. What was also clear was how much Bill hated to be so dependent on others. As soon as he was set in his saddle, Bill whipped his horse around without a word of thanks to either of them and started back to the ranch at a fast gallop.

Longarm turned to Diego. "Round up a few of your best men. We'll need some backup when we go down to palaver."

Diego grunted, hopped onto his horse, and rode for the rocks. Watching him go, Longarm mounted up slowly. He had spoken to Bill with more conviction than he had felt. Still, he reckoned, if this move led to an end to this war, it had to be the right thing....

The Mormon riding out of the canyon toward Longarm and Diego did not look familiar to Longarm, and he struck Longarm as cast from a different mold than that of the elder. There did not seem to be that blazing hostility or sense of righteousness that seemed to govern every glance and motion of Elder Booth.

For this Longarm was grateful, since he had spent a ticklish moment or two approaching the canyon with Diego and the others. The covered wagons had suddenly bristled with rifles, shouts were heard, and some of the wagons were pulled around to make a barrier. For a while Longarm despaired of being able to make it clear that all he wanted was to speak to the person in charge. Only when he waved Diego's men back did the Mormon now approaching mount up and ride out to meet him.

Pulling up before the canyon entrance, Longarm dismounted to wait for the Mormon. The fellow pulled his mount to a halt a few feet in front of Longarm and dismounted. Behind him, crowding the canyon entrance, were about five riflemen, and well beyond them stood the Mormon women, leaning almost gratefully on their shovels and wheelbarrows, watching.

The two men did not shake hands.

"I guess you know which side I'm on," said Longarm.

The Mormon nodded grudgingly. "That's right. The Lazy S. You'd be Mr. Long. I've heard tell of you. My name's Lars. Lars Colburn."

"Too bad we didn't meet when last I visited Little Eden, but I was sent to the elder's restraining room."

"From what I hear, he should have shackled you."

"Why didn't he?"

"The elder said he had not thought it would be necessary." A slight gleam came to Lars's eyes then, as if he appreciated the spectacular manner in which Longarm had shown the elder how much he had underestimated Longarm. "I am sure he knows now he made a mistake."

"Let's get on with this," Longarm said. "I want to propose a deal."

"Go ahead. I'm listening."

"I'm not dealing with you, Lars. Only with the elder."

"I am an elder of the ruling council, a trusted and influential member. I am as interested in the well-being of Little Eden as is Elder Booth."

"But he's the man in charge."

"Yes," snapped Lars.

"Then go get him and bring him out here. In plain sight. He'll be safe. Each of us will be allowed four armed riders at his back to make sure there's no monkey business."

134

"You want me to go back to Little Eden and tell him that?"

"You or someone you send."

"This could be a trick to flush out the elder. Kill him, perhaps. We don't really have to deal, you know. We'll get this dam built in a week, and you don't dare stop us—not with our women in the line of fire."

"That's right. We don't."

"Well, then."

"Wake up, man!" Longarm shot back at him. "What in blazes are you going to do after you get the dam built? Chain your women to it so we don't blow it a second time? And just how long do you think armed men can keep us away? Look what a fine job Cross's men did. This is still Lazy S range, and it's going to stay that way. Now go get him. Tell him the Lazy S is willing to deal."

Lars took a deep breath and looked closely at Longarm. "You speak for the Lazy S owners, do you?"

"For now. Yes."

Lars appeared to hesitate.

"Damn it, Lars. Send someone after the elder before this whole thing blows up in your face!"

The angry sharpness in Longarm's voice shook the man up some. He took a step back, then nodded, even if reluctantly. "I'll go myself," he said. "I should be back here with the elder some time tomorrow morning."

"Diego and I will meet you out there on the flat," Longarm told Lars, pointing. "At noon time. And remember, each of us is allowed only four armed men as backup."

"I understand," Lars said.

"Good."

Longarm turned abruptly, mounted up, and rode back to Diego. Then, with Diego's men shielding them, they wheeled and rode back the way they had come.

• • •

135

The spot Longarm had chosen was little more than a slash of mud now baking in the blistering noonday sun, the stream some couple of hundred yards below them as it cut its new channel out of the raw earth. Already perspiring profusely in the searing heat, Elder Booth swung down out of his saddle and strode toward Longarm, his four armed Mormons remaining on their horses, their rifles resting across their pommels as they peered sullenly out from under the brims of their black hats.

The elder was dressed in black and wore the same kind of wide-brimmed hat as his riders. As he strode closer, his long white beard flowed over one shoulder, while his fierce eyes fixed Longarm malevolently from under his bushy white eyebrows. Noting the grim, unforgiving set to Booth's jaw, Longarm thought of the two men—now dead—he had sent to kill Longarm.

Diego hung back with his men, watching the elder's men carefully as Longarm approached the elder.

"Glad you could make it," Longarm said to Booth.

"Lars said you was willin' to deal. I figure that means you've convinced Bill to accept my offer."

"Hell it does."

"Well, damn it to hell, why'd you bring me up here?"

"I told Lars we were ready to deal. And we are."

"What kind of deal?"

"I think maybe you already know. It's better than you deserve."

The elder's eyes narrowed in expectation. "Go on. Spit it out. I'm listening."

Longarm told him what he had outlined to Bill the day before. When he had finished, Booth's eyes were narrowed in thought as he considered Longarm's offer. Pleased that the elder didn't immediately refuse it, Longarm waited patiently, his arms folded.

At length Booth fixed Longarm with his cold eyes. "Breaking with Cross won't be easy for me."

"Didn't say it would be."

"He will not take kindly to it. He is a mean, unprincipled rattlesnake."

"Is it a deal or isn't it?"

"You will let us rebuild the dam?"

"If you want water."

"And we can use the water as long as we need it?"

"Yes," Longarm said.

"I would like that in writing."

"I'm sure Bill or Sally would be glad to provide that— as soon as you rebuild the dam."

"I'd feel better if I were dealing directly with the owners of the Lazy S."

"Ride with me to their ranch. Now."

This proposal startled the elder. But he seemed eager to take Longarm up on it. "All right, then," he said. "Let's get off this stovetop and start riding."

Longarm went to his horse, the elder to his, and a moment later they rode off, heading in the direction of the Lazy S.

Chapter 12

They rode steadily through the hot afternoon sun and arrived at the Lazy S a few hours before sundown. Not long before they reached the ranch, Longarm became uneasy. A familiar, unsettling smell hung in the air. Less than a mile from the ranch house, they rounded a cliff face and saw, hanging on the horizon just ahead of them, black pillars of smoke pumping skyward. After a hard gallop, they reached the rise in front of the ranch house and pulled up to survey what remained of the Lazy S. Longarm's first thought was that this time Cross's gunslicks had succeeded in burning to the ground not only the barns, but the ranch house as well.

Longarm glanced over at Booth. The elder had already pulled up, his expression revealing the surprise and exasperation he felt. Longarm could almost imagine what he was thinking: Here he was, about to reach an amicable agreement, and Cross had blown it to smithereens.

"I knew nothing at all about this," Booth told Longarm somewhat lamely.

Beside him, Lars Colburn revealed the same dismay. And something else—anger.

Longarm looked back at the devastation below him. "I guess I'll believe you for now," he said, digging his spurs into his mount's flanks.

As he clattered into the smoke-dim compound, Diego and his men close behind, he heard Harry calling to him from behind the cottonwood. Turning his mount in that direction, he loped over and dismounted hurriedly. Diego did the same, but keeping a respectful distance behind. The elder and his men pulled up in the yard and remained mounted.

Harry was lying on the ground propped against the tree, a battered, disheveled Sally lying unconscious on the ground beside him. Her skirt was torn and muddied, her hair a rat's nest, and there was a smudged bruise on her right cheekbone. Harry looked almost as bad. His trousers were still smoking, and there were holes burned into his nightshirt. Both his eyebrows had been scorched off, giving him a wide-eyed, almost innocent look.

As Longarm examined Sally to get some idea of her condition, Harry told him, "It was Sally got me out. If it wasn't for her, I'd still be in there, baked to a crisp." Harry was having difficulty getting his breath, and his lips were stained an unnatural red from blood he had coughed up.

Longarm found Sally's pulse. It was strong, if a little rapid. "How bad is she? What happened to her? She looks like she's been run down."

"She . . . it was the smoke got her. She's been coughing something fierce. She only just passed out."

"Where's Bill?"

"Gone after them."

"What?"

"You should've seen the son of a bitch. Soon's Cross's men rode in, he climbed up out of that wheelchair like a monkey on a string, and he stayed on his horse, pouring lead at them, until they shot his mount out from under him."

"What about the others? Abe? Diego's men?"

"I don't know. They gave a good account of themselves when Cross's men first came on us, but there was just too many of them and too few of us."

Harry began coughing then; not until the paroxysm faded did Longarm ask him how he got hurt.

140

Holding a filthy handkerchief up to his mouth, he said, "I was shooting at them from the window and I kept shooting after they started throwing torches onto the roof. A beam came down in my bedroom and trapped me. That's when Sally came after me. I didn't get back to my senses until she'd finished dragging me out onto the porch."

"How many did you get?"

"Two that I'm sure of, but Cross's men took their wounded back with them when they rode off."

"And you say Bill's gone after them."

Harry nodded weakly. "Cross thought he was dead, or out of action for sure, so they let him be once his horse went down. As soon as they left, he started to wriggle out of that rig he uses. Took him a long time to pull it off his dead horse, but he managed somehow. It was Sally helped him onto another horse, one of Cross's that lost its rider and got left behind. All the time she was bucklin' him onto it, though, she kept tryin' to talk him out of going after Cross, but he wouldn't listen."

Longarm turned to Diego. "Better see about your men—and Abe."

Diego hurried off toward the ruined barn with his men. Longarm watched them go for a moment, then glanced down at the unconscious Sally, wondering if it was her despair at Bill's decision to go after Cross's men as much as the smoke she had inhaled that had caused her to collapse finally. He reckoned her feelings about Bill had turned around some.

He took hold of her shoulder. "Sally," he called, shaking her gently. "Wake up, Sal!"

There was no immediate response. He shook her a couple of times more, calling her name urgently. At last, her eyelids flickered, and when she saw Longarm bent over her, she pushed herself upright and flung herself into his arms, sobbing and coughing with a sudden, shattering violence. Longarm did his best to comfort her, but for a while the only comfort he could offer was his strong arms around her.

At last her crying abated, and, rubbing the soot out of her eyes, she pushed herself away from Longarm and looked up past him at the mounted horsemen staring grimly over at her. Then she recognized the white-bearded figure of Elder Booth. Startled, she sat up quickly and let Longarm help her to her feet.

"You!" she cried, staring at the elder. "What are you doing here?"

Flinching slightly from Sally's angry vehemence, the elder dismounted and strode toward her. With as much dignity as he could muster, he said, "I'm right sorry to see you in this state, ma'am."

"Is that so?" Sally replied defiantly. "Well, sir, thanks for them kind words. If I had a kitchen, I'd invite you in to set and rest a spell—but as you can see, I don't have one! I don't have nothin', 'cause of your partner, Cross!"

"He is a violent, intemperate man," the elder admitted gravely, "but under the circumstances, I must say I cannot blame him. He needs your range and your water supply. He will not survive without it. And I admit, out of necessity, I joined forces with him. But I had nothing to do with this outrage."

"Well, damn it! Ain't he the dog you run with?"

"I have just admitted that. But I repeat, I had no idea he was going to move on you in this fashion. If I had, I would have done my best to dissuade him. Despite the fact that you have stopped the flow of water to my fields, I would not have wished this devastation on you."

Sally was about to reply when Longarm stepped closer. "Sally," he said, "there's no need to continue this. The elder has come here to deal."

Still angry, Sally brushed a lock of damp hair off her forehead. "That's what Bill told me," she snapped, stepping back warily and glancing at Longarm. "But you'll pardon me if I believe any of it after this!"

"I'll speak for myself," said Booth.

"Then do it," Sally said.

Longarm stepped back to let Sally deal with the elder herself, aware suddenly that Sally had grown up some in the past couple of weeks.

Booth cleared his throat. "I'm willin' to go farther than I told Long. I'll rebuild your ranch *and* the dam. In addition, I'll dissolve my partnership with Cross, and stay out of any disputes you may have with him in the future, in return for which you will allow me to rely once again on the diversion dam to feed my irrigated fields in the valley."

"You say you'll rebuild my ranch house?"

The elder nodded emphatically. "As well as the barns and other outbuildings."

"And the dam?" Sally sounded incredulous.

"My people are working on that right now."

Sally turned to Longarm. "What do you think?" she asked, her face flushed with sudden hope.

"I say it is a fair deal, if the elder follows through."

"You have my word, Sally," Booth insisted.

Sally looked back at him. "Better than that, you have my word that if you join up with Cross again, there won't be any water for them fields. The Lazy S can blow that dam as often as you can rebuild it."

"There's no need to repeat the obvious," said Booth stiffly. "I think we understand each other perfectly."

"Then here's my hand on it," Sally said, striding up to the towering, bearded patriarch with her hand out.

Hesitating only momentarily, he reached out and shook her hand firmly.

"Now that that's settled," Longarm said, "how about sending for some men to begin on this ranch."

Booth spun and looked up at Lars Colburn, who was still astride his mount. "Lars, see to it. Ride back to Little Eden and get our best carpenters and loggers."

"Now?"

"You heard me. I want this clearing ringing with the

143

sound of hammers and saws by this time tomorrow."

As Lars galloped off, Booth turned back to Sally.

"I am going to ride back to the dam now, to see how things are progressing and to apprise my people there of this new state of affairs. In the meantime, please try to have some plan ready so the carpenters we send will have something to follow in the rebuilding of the ranch."

Sally just nodded, amazed.

Then Booth turned his full attention on Longarm. "And now, sir, would you mind taking a short walk with me? I'd like a word with you in private."

Longarm shrugged and together the two men walked away from the cottonwood until they were out of earshot of the others. Then the tall, white-bearded elder turned to address Longarm. "You and I still have accounts that need settlin', Long," he rasped angrily. "This bargain I have just struck with the Lazy S has nothing at all to do with my dealings with you. I think it only fair to remind you of that, and I suggest you conduct yourself accordingly."

Longarm smiled back at the glowering elder. "Nice of you to warn me, Booth. But why not let bygones be bygones? I'm sorry about Kristen, but you had no chance of holding onto her. She would never have remained in that harem of yours. Hell, she was never for sale in the first place."

"Kristen was my wife, my Celestial Wife!" Booth fumed, his face darkening above his snow-white beard. "She was the best of the lot! She had more spirit than ten of the others. Together we would have produced lions!"

"Simmer down, Elder. You would never have been sure if they were your lions or your guards'. That's the kind of spirit she had, and that's how she would have gotten back at you. Some animals cannot be tamed."

"You're accusing my guards...!"

"Check around. They got a damn sight more use out of your harem than you did! I figure that's because you were

144

too busy to take care of them, and they were too angry to care if you did. You want to keep a garden full of flowers, mister, you better learn to water and weed them once in a while, or the weeds'll take over."

The tall man groaned at these observations, and Longarm could tell he was fighting desperately not to believe him. But the truth was so obvious, he could not deny it any longer. Torment showed in the man's eyes. If he could have, he would have reached out and throttled Longarm.

"Hell, Booth," Longarm continued easily, "why would I bother to lie to you? How in hell do you figure I got out so easy? Them guards of yours were busy, all right. But they sure as hell weren't busy watching me."

Booth looked about to explode. His mouth worked, but he took a deep breath, and Longarm watched, impressed, as the blind fury in the man slowly died. His eyes sank back into the shadows under his white, beetling brows, and his shaking hand lifted to stroke his long beard. It looked as soft as down and as pure as the driven snow. Longarm figured the man probably spent hours combing it.

"All right, Long," Booth said finally. "What you say has the ring of truth in it. I was a fool, perhaps, to trust my guards and those women. When it comes to certain lusts, no man and no woman can be trusted. I know that. I have wrestled with these same demons myself on occasion. But I repeat what I told you just now. I'll come upon you again, and we'll settle this, once and for all."

"Just so long as you keep this deal you just made with the Lazy S."

"I'll keep it, sir," Booth snapped. "Along with the promise I have just made to you."

Spinning about, he strode back to his horse, flung himself up onto it, and rode off at the head of his three riders.

Longarm watched them ride off, then started for the bunkhouse. He had seen Harry and Sally entering it a moment before.

Peering in, he saw that Sally was hard at work transforming the bunkhouse into more permanent living quarters. Harry was on his feet, helping as best he could. Despite his bedraggled appearance and his leg wound, he looked a lot better to Longarm than he had when they first rode out of Ruby. His cheeks had filled out, his head no longer looked as skeletal as it had, and when he coughed now he did not seem so pitifully racked by it; he seemed capable of withstanding to a much greater extent each powerful paroxysm. More than that, the light in his eyes was steadier now, less hectic, and the faint, feverish flush had vanished from his cheeks. Perhaps this altitude was curing him, Longarm mused—that and Sally's home cooking.

When Sally saw Longarm stooping to enter the bunkhouse, she dropped the mop she was using and turned to him gratefully. "Longarm, if the elder makes good on his promise, it will be wonderful! We'll be all right!"

"I figure he will," said Harry, slumping onto a stool. "He has as much to gain as the Lazy S."

"That's the way I figure it, too," Longarm said. "He thought he could walk right over the Lazy S, but it didn't turn out the way he expected."

"Thanks to you," Sally said.

"What about Abe?" Longarm asked.

"Diego and his men are still looking for him. They haven't come back yet," she said, glancing out the window at the smouldering barn and the brush and trees beyond it.

Longarm shook his head. "And Bill's on his way over to the Cross D to even the score with Dalton Cross. I don't like this. I'm going to have to go after him. How long ago did he leave?"

"An hour, maybe less."

"I wish you could've stopped him."

She sobered instantly. "I couldn't hold him. He was like a madman."

"I might be able to overtake him. He can't ride all that

fast with that rig he's using. He don't complain any, but each mile in that rig is pretty near a torment for him."

She nodded. "I hope you catch him in time."

Longarm touched his hatbrim to her, kept his head low, and ducked out of the bunkhouse. Harry pushed himself off the stool and limped painfully out of the bunkhouse after him.

"Longarm!" he called. "I need to talk to you."

"Make it fast, Harry," Longarm said, turning and waiting for him to catch up.

Glancing back at the bunkhouse to make sure he couldn't be heard, Harry said, "There's something Sally couldn't tell you."

"Go on."

"After she dragged me from the ranch house, they clubbed me to the ground, then took her over to them trees so one of Dalton Cross's hired guns could take his pleasure with her. He was Ham Walsh's brother, and while he raped her, he told her who he was and told her who he was lookin' for. You, Longarm—the one who murdered his brother."

Longarm licked suddenly dry lips. "What's his name?"

"Pete. Pete Walsh. Sally said he repeated his name over and over to her so there wouldn't be any mistake. He's waitin' for you now at Cross's place. That's what he told her. He wants you to come after him."

"What kind of horse is he ridin'?"

"A black. He don't look at all like his brother. He's a thin, mean-lookin' son of a bitch, dressed in a black suit. He wore a white shirt, for Christ's sake, and never got it dirty."

"How much of this did Bill see?"

Harry looked very unhappy. "All of it. He was caught in that rig on the ground beside the dead horse, screamin' at them, until one of Cross's men came over and slugged him with the barrel of his Colt."

"No wonder Bill went after them."

Longarm looked past Harry at the bunkhouse. He thought he could see Sally's back through the dirt-encrusted window as she attacked the floor with her wet mop. "Does Sally know you're tellin' me all this?"

Harry nodded. "She knows why I followed you out of the bunkhouse. She wanted to warn you about this fellow Pete. But she's too ashamed about it to tell you herself."

Longarm nodded grimly. He could understand perfectly her shame and her anger. At that moment he shared it. "I'm worried about Abe," Longarm told Harry. "See what you can do to help Diego find him. I sure as hell hope he's not hurt bad."

Harry nodded. "Sure thing, Longarm."

Longarm strode over to his horse, stepped into his saddle, and swung his horse around. He left the ruined, still smouldering compound at a hard gallop.

Dalton Cross could hardly believe his eyes. He had just got back from trashing the Lazy S, had seen to his wounded men—all but Jimmy Craddock had suffered only minor flesh wounds—washed up, and told his woman to put on the supper. Now here came that fool Adams strapped in that crazy rig. They'd shot one horse out from under him and Lem Shanks had clubbed him senseless, but here was the poor stupid bastard riding in, as big as life and twice as nasty. The first time they had taken his legs; this time they just might take his head off.

Cross went back inside for his rifle, then reappeared on the veranda. As he waited, one leg up on the veranda railing, he called across the yard to Burt and Lem, who were on their way into the barn. Cross had no idea where Pete was—probably in the bunkhouse, scaring up a poker game.

Burt and Lem turned to see what he wanted. Cross pointed. They glanced toward the gate and saw Adams riding past the windmill on his way into the compound.

"That son of a bitch's crazy!" cried Lem, his big, long

148

face comical as he gaped at the closing rider.

"Go get Pete and Jeeter!" Cross called. "This poor slob is askin' for it."

"It's what Pete did to his missus, I bet," said Lem.

"Never mind that. Get the others."

With long, awkward strides, Lem broke from his companion and headed for the bunkhouse. Cross levered a fresh cartridge into his Winchester and smiled. Bill Adams was well within range now. Cross could pick him off as easy as a fly on an adobe wall. But that would be awkward. The poor sap would be flopping all over the horse, and it would be devilishly difficult to get him down out of that crazy rig. Hell, the goddamn horse might bolt.

The uncanny thing about it was Bill's silence. The man said nothing as he stared at Cross and kept riding. He didn't even have a gun out as he rode, but he was looking about the compound—for some sign of Pete Walsh, Cross figured.

Then Pete and the rest of the Cross D riders streamed suddenly from the bunkhouse. Walsh was in the lead, striding eagerly toward Bill, his sixgun out and ready. As soon as Bill Adams saw him, he turned his horse to ride straight for him and drew his own sidearm. Those standing behind Pete scattered. Pete laughed as Adams experienced some difficulty keeping his mount to a steady trot. Aiming carefully, Pete fired once. The horse came down like a tree crashing in a forest. It thrashed once or twice, then lay still. Bill was pinned under it.

Still striding forward, Pete fired a second time, and the gun Adams had finally managed to draw went spinning bloodily from his hand. He bent forward then and tried to drag his rifle from the saddle boot, but it was jammed too tightly under the dead horse.

By that time, the smirking Pete Walsh was standing over Adams. Bill reached up to grab him. Stepping back, Pete kicked out with his right foot, catching Bill on the side of the head. The man slumped over, unconscious. Holstering

149

his sixgun, Pete glanced over at Cross.

"You got a wheelchair?"

"What the hell do you want that for?"

"You got one?"

"No."

"How about a baby carriage?"

"A what?"

"Okay. How about a wheelbarrow?"

"Sure, I got a wheelbarrow."

"Send someone for it. We got ourselves a circus here."

Cross told Burt Hoover to get the wheelbarrow and Burt was off like a shot. Cross left the porch and walked over to see what Pete Walsh was up to. Pulling up alongside the dead horse, he saw that Pete had his pocket knife out and was slicing through the leather straps that held the stumps of Adams's legs to the stirrup. It didn't take him long to free up Adams. Pete straightened up and the rest of the men took hold of Adams and pulled him unceremoniously off the saddle.

He was just beginning to come around when Burt Hoover returned with the wheelbarrow.

"Tie him into it," Pete said to one of the men beside him, "and someone else get me a horse and a long rope."

"You mind telling me what the Christ you're up to?" Cross asked Pete.

Grinning, Pete glanced over at Cross. "This poor stupid son of a bitch still thinks he's a man. He don't know yet that he's licked. Finished. Hell, he ain't even worth a bullet. When I get through with him, he'll realize what he is. That'll take the sting out of him."

Cross understood at once. Damn good idea. Shooting Bill Adams might cause trouble up here—from the elder, especially. This way, he'd let the poor son of a bitch live, but with his balls torn out. He'd be like putty after that, and no harm to a soul.

"Go to it, you crazy bastard," Cross said, grinning appreciatively at Pete Walsh. "Maybe I should've made you my foreman instead of your brother."

"Ramrodding ain't my game, Cross," Pete said as someone handed him a rope. "This here's my speed." Mounting up, he grinned with amusement down at Bill Adams, who by this time was trussed like a turkey to the bed of the wheelbarrow. Tossing one end of the rope to Lem Shanks, he said, "Tie this end to the wheelbarrow, in the middle."

Lem didn't quite know what Pete wanted. Immediately another Cross rider, grinning, snatched the rope from him and wrapped it around the handles, contriving to make the rope trail back to Pete from the center of the wheelbarrow.

"Try that!" the fellow said.

Pete yanked on the rope. The handles lifted and the wheelbarrow moved a few feet across the compound.

Pete took out his sixgun. "Now, don't hit the damn fool," he cried. "Just scare the shit out of him. I want him to shit in his pants till that wheelbarrow's full."

He sent a shot over Bill's slumped figure. Adams came awake, a startled look on his face. At once Pete turned and spurred across the compound, the wheelbarrow flying after him, the frantic, gaping Adams hanging on for dear life. With a roar of laughter, the rest of the men took out their sixguns and began sending rounds just over the plunging wheelbarrow and the frantic man tied inside.

Watching them blasting away for a moment, Cross ducked back to the veranda to get his rifle, a broad grin on his face.

It was about an hour before sundown when Longarm came within sight of the Cross D. He had not been able to overtake Bill, and Longarm's hope was that he had somehow managed to pass him, which would put him between Bill and the Cross D ranch. But it was a forlorn hope at best, and he was riding out of a thick stand of cottonwood, approaching the rear of the biggest horse barn, when he heard the shots. They came from the compound beyond the barn.

Longarm dug his spurs into his mount. Once he reached the rear of the big horse barn, he snatched his rifle from its scabbard and leaped from the still moving animal. As the horse pulled up and trotted away, Longarm ran the remaining distance to the rear corral, clambered through the log fencing, and darted inside the barn through the back door. He pushed a pile of hay aside and peered through the window to get a clear, unobstructed view of the compound and the big ranch house beyond.

What he saw turned his stomach.

A rider fitting the description Harry had given him of Pete Walsh was dragging a wheelbarrow containing the trussed figure of Bill Adams back and forth across the yard, while Cross and his hired guns took potshots at the terrified Bill. Longarm did not know what to do at first. He considered shooting Pete Walsh out of his saddle, but was afraid that this would put Bill in even greater danger.

Then Bill solved his dilemma. Somehow managing to get his arms free, Bill suddenly leaned forward and grabbed the rope attached to the wheelbarrow in a desperate effort to yank Pete Walsh off his mount. It had little effect on Walsh, who quickly wheeled his horse, charged back past the wheelbarrow, and yanked it viciously around. Bill went spilling out of it, hitting the ground hard enough to cause Longarm to wince, then tumbling awkwardly as he struggled to get upright, his two stumps flailing helplessly.

The firing at Bill had stopped by this time. Laughing heartily, Pete Walsh turned his horse again and rode straight at Bill, who by this time had managed to push himself up onto his stumps. A grin on his face, Pete Walsh began firing just over Bill's head as he charged straight at Bill. Screaming pain with each step he took on his raw, bloodied stumps, Bill fled desperately before his tormentor. Leaving behind a bloody trail, he waddled frantically across the compound.

Still firing, Walsh thundered closer. In a desperate attempt to escape, Bill veered suddenly toward the barn. But

Walsh, not intending to hurt Bill, turned in the same direction. In that single terrible instant, Bill scrambled directly into the horse's path. He did not cry out. The only sound was that of the horse's hooves thudding into his body.

Cross and his gunslicks stood silently, their guns lowered, as they watched the bloody piece of what had once been Bill Adams kick free of the hard-driving hooves.

Chapter 13

A stricken silence fell over Cross's men as they stared across the yard at Bill's body. Even Pete Walsh appeared affected by what he had done. His face pale with shock, he pulled up and swung his horse back around again, then dismounted, one hand still holding tightly to his reins, his smoking gun in his hand. Dalton Cross looked as grim as the rest, and took a few cautious steps toward the crumpled body, his men moving forward with the same awed deliberation.

Levering a fresh cartridge into his Winchester, Longarm left the window and flung himself prone in the barn's open doorway. Raising his rifle to his shoulder, he sighted along the barrel at Pete Walsh and announced his presence with a single curt demand.

"All of you! Drop your guns!"

Every man spun in his direction, but not one had the sense to do as he requested. Walsh swung up his sixgun and fired, but his hammer came down on an empty chamber. As hot lead from two of Cross's men bit into the ground in front of him and chewed away at the doorframe, Longarm fired at Pete. But Pete was ducking back to his horse, and Longarm missed. As he levered in a fresh round, Pete Walsh leapt onto his horse and galloped away, his head down over the horse's neck, his ass riding high. Ignoring the bullets slamming into the ground and barn, Longarm swung around and aimed at the base of the horse's tail, hoping for a spine shot—or, if his round carried high, the rider's back.

He fired. The horse kept going. He swore, levered, and fired again. Walsh and his horse disappeared into a swale, heading for a distant line of cottonwoods.

By this time the rest of Cross's men were pouring a steady rattle of fire at Longarm. Crabbing sideways to the frame of the barn's doorway, he went prone again and carefully returned the gunslicks' hasty fire. One man lost his gun hand along with his sixgun; another went bowling back against the bunkhouse wall, coughing blood. But it was Dalton Cross Longarm was searching for with his gun barrel.

He caught sight of him behind a corner of the ranch house, frantically reloading his rifle. Longarm placed two quick .44 slugs into the woodwork inches from the corner, then waited, but Cross remained flat against the wall. Pushing himself back into the shadow of the barn door, Longarm took out his sixgun, tracked a gunslick darting out from behind the blacksmith's shed, and winged him. As the wounded man sprawled forward, crying out, Cross poked his head out from the corner and looked in that direction.

His finger resting on the trigger of his rifle, Longarm took a deep breath. Cross, gaining more courage with each passing second, moved farther away from the side of the house, peering around now at the compound, wondering perhaps if Longarm had run out. The compound grew silent as Cross's men waited for Longarm's next shot to tell them where he was. Longarm waited until Cross's entire left shoulder was exposed before squeezing the trigger.

The man went flying backward, clutching at his shattered shoulder. At that moment Longarm heard something behind him and whirled. A tall, grizzled gunslick was rushing at him from the back of the barn, a pitchfork in his hand. Longarm flung up his Colt and fired twice. The first shot caught the man in the chest, the second in the groin. Longarm rolled swiftly to one side as the wounded man, still carrying the pitchfork, staggered past him out into the compound. A fusillade of shots from his nervous bunkmates riddled his body and he collapsed like a piece of bloody pudding close to where Bill Adams had come to rest.

"Cross!" Longarm cried. "Can you hear me?"

"What do you want, you bastard?" came Cross's response. He had crawled away from the house and was crouching behind an overturned grindstone near an outhouse.

"Your army of gunslicks is melting away. Diego and his men should have circled around your ranch by now, and they're moving in. I'm willing to show you a way out of this if you'll throw your gun down and tell your men to do the same."

"A way out? What're you talkin' about?"

"Throw your rifle away and I'll tell you."

"Damn it to hell, man! I'm wounded bad. You busted up my shoulder."

"It could've been a lot worse, Cross. And it will be if you don't do what I say!"

"All right! All right!" he cried.

Longarm saw his arm fly up as he flung his rifle out from behind the grindstone.

"Throw out your sidearm, too!"

It landed a few feet from the rifle.

"Now stand up and step out where I can see you."

"Jesus! How do I know you won't shoot me down in cold blood?"

"You'll have to trust me."

"Damn it! I don't know anything about you! How can I trust you?"

At that moment some of Cross's men smashed through the windowpanes in the bunkhouse with their weapons and began peppering the barn's entrance. Bullets skidded through the hay beside Longarm. Longarm pushed himself closer to the door and pumped about five quick slugs through the windows, shattering what glass remained in them, effectively silencing the men inside.

"Cross!" Longarm called. "I'm a deputy U.S. marshal out of Denver. If I tell you to trust me, you can. If you don't, I'll do what I can to bring you in, one way or another. I got no warrant for you or your hired killers, but I can sure as hell scare one up if I need to. I'm willing to let you get out of this with your hide. But I won't wait much longer!"

There was a shocked silence at Longarm's announcement of who he was, broken finally by Cross's weak voice. "All right. I heard you. I'm comin' out!"

Slowly, the man stood up in plain view and walked haltingly out into the front yard. Once he was in clear sight, he halted and looked around at his men.

"Drop your guns!" he told them. "It's all over. I'm shot bad!"

Even as he spoke, Cross sagged weakly to the ground. Slowly, warily, like wild animals coming in from the woods, Cross's remaining force of gunslicks stepped from cover.

Longarm stepped out of the barn and came to a halt in plain sight, not more than twenty yards from Cross. "Tell them to throw their rifles, sidearms, and gunbelts into a pile near Bill's body."

"You heard him!" rasped Cross.

The men slunk forward and did as they were told.

"And get those heroes in the bunkhouse out here," Longarm snapped.

Three men went into it and a moment later came back out, helping three badly wounded men. Two others, bandaged sloppily, followed them out. Watching them, Longarm realized he could not trust a single one of them. He kept his rifle leveled on Cross.

"Listen carefully, Cross. I won't repeat it."

"Go ahead, for Christ's sake! I'm bleedin' to death!"

"Get out of the Rubies. Now. And take your army with you. Elder Booth has made his peace with the Lazy S, and I've got enough on you right now for a federal warrant that will chase you clear to South America. Go now and I'll let you round up your stock and take whatever you can fit in a wagon. That's the best I can do."

"How much time've I got?"

"Five days."

"Jesus Christ! That don't give me hardly no time at all."

"At the end of the fifth day, if I don't see smoke rising from this compound, I'll come for you—warrant or no warrant."

"Smoke?"

"That's right. Smoke. You like to burn things, I notice. When I see that smoke, it'll mean you've set fire to this here ranch house and barn—that you're on the way out of the Rubies. Count your blessings, Cross. You'll be a free man—until you stick your fist in another cookie jar and find you can't get it out."

Cross clutched at his bleeding shoulder as he thought over Longarm's demands. At length, he raised his eyes and looked bleakly at Longarm.

"All right, damn you. It's a deal."

"Good. Now have two of your men hitch up a wagon and put Bill's body in it. I'll want them to drive Bill home to the Lazy S and bury him. I'll be escorting them."

"Where's . . . that sheepherder and his men?" Cross asked, looking nervously over his shoulder.

"Where you can't see them."

It was getting on to dusk by this time. Longarm saw Cross peer nervously around, shiver, then bark out the names of two men and tell them what he wanted. As the men moved reluctantly past Longarm, heading for the barn, one of Cross's men who had ducked back into the shadows of a tool shed went for a sidearm he had kept hidden in his belt. Longarm swung his rifle and squeezed off a shot. The fellow went slamming back against the shed, dropping his gun. Then, staring in surprise at Longarm, he slid down the wall, leaving a bloody track on the weathered boards.

"Anyone else?" Longarm called.

A few men shook their heads quickly. Others stepped back, watching him fearfully. Longarm walked over to the pile of firearms and kicked the sidearms and gunbelts into a pile, then looked over at Cross.

"Let's make this clear, Cross. I get any more unpleasantness from your men, the next round will finish you off first. Just so I'll be sure."

"You heard 'im, boys!" Cross rasped desperately, the blood pouring through his fingers as he clutched miserably at his shoulder. "Damn it! Don't any of you try nothin'! It's all over here. Finished!"

Longarm saw the men slump wearily, the fight oozing out of them. Cross was their paycheck, their room and board. If he said it was over, it was.

"Good," said Longarm dryly. "Now take your men over to the bunkhouse out of harm's way. In this darkness, Diego's men might get careless and start shooting at shadows. It'll give you a chance to see to your wound."

"Right now?"

"Now!"

Without further protest, the Cross D owner struggled to his feet and led his men back into the bunkhouse.

Fifteen minutes later, with Longarm riding escort, the two men Cross had selected drove a flatbed wagon containing Bill Adams's body from the Cross D compound on its way back to the Lazy S.

It was Abe who greeted them when they reached the Lazy S early the next day. He held a Colt in his right hand and was leaning on a makeshift crutch tucked into his left armpit. There was a clean, tightly wrapped bandage around the calf of his left leg, but he looked vigorous enough as he swung closer, his eyes fixed on the two Cross D men. It was clear he recognized them.

"Hold your fire, Abe," Longarm called. "I've brought these two along to help out. Bill's in the wagon. Dead."

Abe pulled up at this news and leaned heavily, wearily on his crutch, his eyes bleak as he peered up at Longarm. "Can't say as I'm surprised, from what Harry told me."

The wagon was alongside Abe by that time. Longarm

160

motioned for the two Cross D men to hold up. The driver hauled back on the reins, and Abe swung over to the wagon to glance in. Shocked, he looked up at Longarm for an explanation.

"I'll explain later," Longarm told him wearily. "Have these two put Bill in a box soon's you can. I don't want Sally seeing him like this. We'll bury him this afternoon in the high pasture out there beyond the barn, near them trees."

Abe followed Longarm's gaze and nodded.

"Have any of the elder's men shown up yet?" Longarm asked.

"No, they ain't. And I'll believe it when I see it."

"Well, these two here will be helping us out for the next week or so. See they don't have too much idle time on their hands."

Abe nodded. "I'll see to it," he said. With astonishing agility, he swung up onto the seat beside the two men, his sidearm resting on his lap, the bore yawning up at the man on the seat next to him.

As Abe directed the wagon toward the pasture, Longarm rode on into the Lazy S compound. Harry appeared in the bunkhouse doorway and said something to Sally inside. She poked her head out eagerly, but her face fell the moment she saw the look on Longarm's face. Then she caught sight of the wagon moving past the burnt-out shell of the barn.

"Longarm," she asked, her voice soft with dread, "what's in that wagon?"

Longarm dismounted in front of the bunkhouse. He felt incredibly weary. Watching over Bill's corpse and his two unhappy companions through the night had not allowed him much sleep.

"Bill," he told her. "Bill's in that wagon."

She darted from the doorway, heading after the wagon. In two quick strides Longarm overtook her and spun her around. "Stay away from Bill," he told her. "He wouldn't want you to see him like he is now. We'll box him up pronto, then bury him, and that'll be the end of it."

161

"I want to see him!"

"Why?"

"Because..." She halted, confused, tears streaming down her face.

"There's no reason, and you know it. You told me how you felt about Bill. You meant it, and if you didn't have the guts to tell him to his face, he knew what you felt. So give him this much, at least. Let us box him up and lower him into the ground and say goodbye, and when we've got that done, try to remember the man who once stood tall enough to come out here with you—and who loved you."

Covering her face with her hands, she collapsed, sobbing, into his arms. He held her for a while, then gently guided her back to the bunkhouse. Harry was waiting in the doorway for her. He took her from Longarm and helped her inside.

Following in after Harry, Longarm asked, "Where's Diego?"

"He and his people have gone back to their flocks. He says they're scattered all over the Rubies by now. He's sorry, but he and his people must go after them."

Longarm nodded. He understood perfectly.

On the way back from Bill's burial the next morning, their two unhappy gravediggers in front so Abe could keep an eye on them, Longarm sighted the first wagonload of workers sent by Elder Booth. By the time they reached the bunkhouse, a line of seven covered wagons had already topped the ridge above the ranch and were heading down the swale toward the ranch compound.

"Well, dunk me in sheep dip and call me Sweetie," Abe drawled, his old eyes gleaming. "If that don't beat all. You got that elder to dance to our tune, after all."

"Looks like it," said Longarm. "Do me a favor, Abe. Rope me the best horse you've got. I have some hard riding ahead of me."

"Sure. I'll get you the black," Abe told him, and swung

off to the lower pasture, where most of the Lazy S's horses had been herded into a rope corral.

Sally led the way into the bunkhouse out of the heat. The former Cross D riders shuffled in unhappily and found a place in the corner. They were dirty and smelled of fresh earth. They would be gone at the first opportunity, Longarm realized. If they did, and made it back to the Cross D, what they would have to tell Cross would only harden the wounded man's resolve to light out.

"I'm just as surprised as Abe," Harry said, stationing himself at the window and peering out at the oncoming wagons. "We sure must have convinced Booth we mean to stand our ground."

"Well, there's no sense rubbing it in," Longarm replied. "I figure it might be a good idea if you and Sally went out there and welcomed them."

"Of course," said Sally, her face brightening somewhat at the prospect.

"Sure," said Harry.

"Good. Then I elect you and Harry to take charge of the greeting committee," Longarm replied.

"What about you, Longarm?"

"There's two places I might find Pete Walsh. Ruby or Ely City. I'll try Ruby first, then Ely City."

"Is Pete Walsh the one who . . . ?"

"Killed Bill?"

Sally nodded.

"Yes. But maybe you could say it was Bill himself, riding in like that without any backup. Or maybe it was the liquor set him afire. Or maybe he loved you too much and wanted to prove he was still able to punish any man who shamed you. It's all of that, I guess, or maybe none of it—with Pete Walsh at the end of it."

Sally frowned as she swallowed the truth of what Longarm had just suggested, then tossed her hair back off her shoulder and peered up at him closely. "When will you be ridin' out then?"

"As soon as Abe brings me a fresh horse."

"That soon?"

"Yes."

"Hey, what about me?" said Harry. "My leg's comin' along fine. I'm well enough to side you. Ain't that right, Sally?"

"I guess so," she admitted, somewhat reluctantly.

Longarm shook his head. "No, Harry. I want you to stay here and look after things with Abe. Besides," he added, "looks to me like this altitude agrees with you."

Harry nodded, glancing quickly at Sally. "I am feelin' a whole lot better, and that's the truth."

Longarm looked out the window. "The Mormons'll be in the yard soon. Go out there now and make them welcome. Looks like your feud with the elder is all patched up."

As Harry and Sally hurried from the bunkhouse, Longarm looked over at the two men he'd borrowed from Dalton Cross and told them to get off their asses and join the welcoming committee. They lurched to their feet and scuttled from the bunkhouse. The low-ceilinged bunkhouse smelled better almost instantly.

Longarm went over to the wood stove, lifted off a pot of hot coffee, and poured himself a cup. Then he slumped wearily down at the table and sipped it. Soon the sound of hearty, even friendly voices came through the open door to him.

He heard the heavy tread of booted feet suddenly and looked up. Lars Colburn stooped low as he entered the bunkhouse. Once inside, he straightened to his full height, squaring his impressive shoulders. He looked a good deal taller than Longarm remembered, his head back and his eyes gleaming with an authority he had not shown before this. Striding over to Longarm, he halted before the table and gazed down at Longarm, his expression grim.

"Have some coffee," Longarm said. "There's plenty in the pot."

"Thank you, no."

164

Sipping his coffee, Longarm waited. It was plain as the eyes on a raccoon's face that Lars had something important to tell him.

"Sally Adams told me you were in here—and she also mentioned the death of her husband."

"That was Cross's work, or one of his men."

"I know, and I am sorry Bill's dead. I understand he was a good friend of yours. You have my condolences."

Longarm looked up at Lars curiously. "Thanks."

"I want to assure you that the deal you made for the Lazy S with Elder Booth will be kept."

Leaning back in his chair, Longarm said, "I assumed it would. I never doubted the elder's word, once he saw what he was up against."

"The council of elders has voted Elder Booth out of leadership. I am now the head elder. Booth's harem has been turned into a school. His wives have been freed. The Saints in Nevada will no longer be outcasts because of this practice, and Elder Booth has been driven out of Little Eden, along with those few Destroying Angels who remained loyal to him."

"Driven out?"

Elder Colburn's mouth became a hard, unrelenting line. "Yes."

"Pretty drastic treatment for losing an election, wouldn't you say?"

"Times change and men better change with them, or be trampled into dust by the steeds of history," Lars replied coldly. "Brigham Young is dead, and we in Little Eden have no desire to resurrect him in the person of Elder Booth."

"Just why are you telling me all this?"

"To warn you. The elder blames you for his being cast out, and has vowed to kill you."

"Oh," Longarm said, downing his coffee and getting to his feet, "is that all?"

"Mr. Long, I suggest you take Elder Booth's vow seriously."

165

"Why are you still calling him Elder Booth if you've driven him out?"

"Habit, I guess."

"Yeah. Well, I got a habit of staying alive, so don't worry about me none, Elder Colburn. Thanks, anyway."

Longarm stepped outside then, Lars following after him. The compound was pretty well clogged with covered wagons, their traces filled with unhappy mules the teamsters found impossible to quiet. Maybe it was the altitude. Sally and Harry were moving among the Mormon workers, showing their appreciation and doing their best to make everyone feel welcome. There were only a few Mormon women, Longarm noticed. The rest, he realized, were probably back at the dam, breaking their backs pushing wheelbarrows loaded with dirt and dragging oversized logs into place, like upright beasts of burden.

Longarm saw Abe pushing through the crowd, leading the black he had promised him. It was already saddled. Abe had tied Longarm's bedroll and bag to the cantle.

Pulling to a halt in front of Longarm, Abe grinned wistfully. "Wish I was goin' with you," he told Longarm. "The Lazy S is gettin' too damn crowded for this old cowpoke. If I didn't have this busted leg, I'd be ridin' alongside you. If you'd have me, that is."

"I'd be glad to have you siding me, Abe," Longarm replied, smiling at the bowed old campaigner, "but right now I'm counting on you to keep an eye on things here. Tell Sally and Harry I'll be back in about four days to check on whether or not Cross is keeping his promise to pull out. I'll see you then."

Stepping up into his saddle, Longarm nodded curtly to Lars Colburn, wheeled the black, and rode off. Glancing over at Sally as he left the compound, he saw her looking after him, her face registering concern and disappointment. She probably had counted on a few parting words with him, Longarm realized, but he had decided not to interrupt her and Harry.

Chapter 14

Ryan, the Ruby Saloon's barkeep, assured Longarm that Pete Walsh had not shown up in Ruby and suggested Longarm try Ely City. It was about what Longarm had expected, and he reached Ely City late that same night. The desk clerk recognized him at once as the naked guest who had shot down two gunmen not long before, and he watched wide-eyed as Longarm mounted the steps to his room.

He slept that night with the back of a chair jammed up against the doorknob, crumpled newspaper between his bed and the door, and a loaded .44 under his pillow. It seemed to do the trick. It was the noise of a bustling town below his window that woke him the following morning, not a crazed gunman breaking through the door.

Longarm ate a leisurely breakfast, then indulged himself at the barber, enjoying a steaming bath followed by a shave and a haircut. Afterwards, he visited a men's furnishing store and bought himself a fresh shirt, string tie, and clean stockings, discarded the old and donned the new, then strolled down the street to the Silver Slipper, where Kristen told him she had once worked.

The gambling saloon was only just stirring to life, but already the bar was filling up with odd sorts downing a quick one to keep them going until mid-afternoon, when they could really begin to tank up. Many of the bar's patrons were merchants of the town, but most were the miners and prospectors who had already made enough from their diggings to say goodbye to tents and sluice boxes and were now doing their best to drink and gamble through their fortunes so they could return once again to back-breaking, honest toil.

Or so it seemed to Longarm as he asked the barkeep for Sam Feeley, then bought himself a bottle and found a quiet table in a corner. Still nursing his first drink, Longarm saw a short, beefy man with red hair leave his private office near the bar and head for his table. He was dressed in green trousers, white shirt and vest, no hat, and a townsman's shoes. This had to be Sam Feeley, Longarm guessed, as he finished his drink and leaned back in his chair to await the saloon owner.

"You don't look like a drummer," Freeley said as he stopped at Longarm's table and gazed down at him.

"I'm not a drummer."

"Mike said you wanted to see me."

"He was right. Join me in a drink?"

"I might sell that bilge, but I sure as hell don't drink it," Feeley said.

"It didn't taste much like Maryland rye, at that."

"I'm a busy man. What business do you have with me?"

"I'm looking for someone. Pete Walsh."

"You a lawman?"

"Yeah. But right now I'm on a vacation."

"This Walsh a friend of yours, is he?"

"Not so you'd notice."

"Last I heard he was dealing faro at the Gold Nugget. That was a few weeks ago, though."

Longarm nodded. "Then you ain't seen him around town lately."

"The Silver Slipper takes up most of my wakin' hours, mister."

"There's someone else I'm looking for. Her name's Kristen. She said she once worked for you."

"If you can wait until five, she'll be in. She's workin' for me again. Deals blackjack till midnight."

"I can't wait that long. Maybe you know where she's staying."

"I'd like to tell you, but I can't."

"Why not?"

Sam Feeley pulled out a chair and sat down, looking Longarm up and down as recognition flooded his face. He leaned suddenly forward in his chair. "Say, you mind telling me who you are?"

"Name's Custis Long. My friends call me Longarm."

"Damn! I should've known who you was."

"How come?"

"Kristen told me all about you. Said for me to keep an eye peeled in case you showed. Ain't you the one killed them two Destroyin' Angels who was after her? The same gent what boiled out of the hotel after one of them stark naked."

Longarm smiled coldly. "Where's Kristen staying?"

"In a roomin' house behind the hotel. She ain't usin' her real name, though."

"What name's she using?"

"Molly Smith."

"She in trouble, is she?"

"It's that crazy son of a bitch, Booth—the one used to be in charge of that Mormon settlement—that's after her. He's livin' in a big abandoned mansion north of town. It's been a home for bats long as I can remember, but Booth's moved in, so I hear. He's got four of his night riders with him, a passel of wives, and a brood of howling brats he took with him when he was booted out of his settlement."

"Has he built himself a pool out there?"

"A what?"

"Never mind."

"Anyway, he's come in here twice now with blood in is eye, lookin' for Kristen," Feeley went on.

"He ain't asked you to fire her again, has he?"

The man swallowed. "Kristen told you about that, did she?"

"Yes, she did."

"Well, that time was different. Booth ain't the head of a whole community. He's just one more Saint lookin' for a woman. Anyway, Kristen is certain sure he's goin' to kidnap her soon's he gets the chance. That's why she's been hopin' you'd show up."

"Which street is that rooming house on?"

"Second Street, number 24, on a corner. Three stories high, white with blue trim."

Longarm finished his drink. "Thanks. Think I'll go see her."

"You better wait a while."

"Why? It's almost noon."

Feeley grinned. "At this hour you'll have to dynamite the place to get in. The girls in this particular roomin' house don't rest much at night, so they have to make up for it by sleepin' most of the day."

"What's the name of the madam runs the place?"

"Josie Montana."

"New in town?"

"Yep. Keeps a clean place and clean girls. She don't advertise. And that's because she don't need to."

"Wouldn't want to bother her then. I'll finish my bottle and go see her later. Thanks, Feeley."

"My friends call me Sam," he said, brushing his thinning red hair back off his forehead and pulling his chair closer to the table.

Longarm leaned back in his chair and poured himself another drink without asking Feeley to join him. "If I don't get a chance to see Kristen this afternoon," he told Feeley, "you tell her I'll be in tonight."

"Sure thing, Long."

Longarm said nothing more. He lifted his drink and tossed

it down. The saloon owner realized he had been dismissed. With a nervous smile, he pushed himself to his feet and moved back to his office through the rapidly filling saloon. Already a couple of poker games were in progress and Longarm thought he might sit in on a game for a while, before taking a ride out to visit Elder Booth.

He would see to Pete Walsh later.

Meanwhile, as far as Longarm was concerned, it was about time Booth stopped hounding Kristen. Maybe Longarm could convince the old white-beard to be satisfied with what was left of his harem.

The four Destroying Angels were passing a jug around on the mansion's front porch when Longarm rode up. The men did not look at all like angels, nor did they appear capable of destroying anything more ferocious than the flies buzzing about them. They needed shaves, haircuts, and baths. Their shirts and vests were stained, their pants ragged and dusty. Even the weapons on their hips looked dirty and poorly kept. Once these men had been mighty—the dark, unchallenged force behind Elder Booth's power. Now they were just dirty, unkempt misfits.

As he dismounted in front of the porch and tramped up the porch steps, the one nearest the door loomed upright, squared his shoulders unhappily, then moved over to block Longarm's path. His stomach sagged out over his gunbelt, and the stench of valley tan on his breath was so strong, Longarm wondered if he were not using it as a gargle.

"What you want?" the man growled.

"Booth in?"

"Who's askin'?"

Longarm reached out, grabbed the man's shoulder, and spun him back toward his companions. He tripped and went down heavily, crashing into them as they went for their guns. Laughing, Longarm drew his Colt. A peaceful look came over their faces as they stepped hastily back and lifted their hands from their holsters.

"We don't want no trouble, mister," the fellow Longarm had pushed aside told him as he struggled to his feet.

"Good. All of you, throw your sidearms over the porch railing."

As soon as they had done what Longarm told them, he asked where Booth was.

"He's out back," one of them told Longarm. "You want me to get him?"

"No. What I want is for you four to start walking. Toward town. Double back, or try anything foolish, and I'll make you walk barefoot all the way."

"Hey!" one of them pleaded. "At least let us get our horses."

"Walk now or I'll make you dance."

As Longarm spoke, he aimed his revolver at the men's feet. They needed no more urging. As they scrambled off the porch, Longarm bent, picked their jug of valley tan up off the porch, and flung it at them.

"Here!" he cried.

The last one off the porch turned, saw the jug in mid-air, and made a remarkable catch. Before he relinquished it to his friends, he took several enormous gulps. Longarm watched them weave off down the road for a moment or two, then descended the porch steps and walked around to the rear of the large, dilapidated mansion. It had possibilities, perhaps, but it still needed considerable repair. There were holes in the roof—the entrance, he guessed, for those bats Sam Feeley had mentioned.

Rounding the corner of the building, he saw seven or eight dirty children, boys and girls mixed, tearing around an outhouse after a terrified pig. The children were filthy; their clothing was torn and none of them wore shoes. Their hair and faces there wore as much mud as the pig they were chasing.

They were trying to catch it for supper, perhaps, but the

pig was determined to live another day. As the wild, shriek-
ing torrent of brats tore after the desperate animal, their
cries rose to a crescendo that made Longarm shudder.

Rounding a small shed, Longarm saw Elder Booth standing on the back porch with a shotgun in his hand.

"You son of a bitch!" he cried. "I saw you ridin' up!"

"Did you, now."

"You chased off them useless assholes, but you ain't
scarin' me."

Longarm took a cautious step toward the porch, hoping
to talk some sense into the elder, or at least stall the man
long enough to give Longarm a chance to draw on him.

At that moment the pig scooted out from under a bush
and ducked between Longarm's legs, almost knocking him
over. The screaming urchins chasing the pig slammed into
him. With a triumphant squeal, the pig doubled back and
headed for the porch, shooting up the steps like a loose
cannon ball, the pack of howling kids pounding after it.

The elder skipped quickly to one side, cursing at the kids
and lifting his shotgun out of their path. At once Longarm
had his Colt out and was leveling it on the elder, while the
kids, screeching at the top of their lungs, chased the pig
through the elder's legs, then over the railing.

"Drop that shotgun, Booth," Longarm told him.

"I'll roast in hell first!" Booth cried, firing point-blank
at Longarm.

Longarm had already flung himself to the ground. He
struck it hard and was rolling to one side when the double
load of buckshot whistled over his head. At that moment
the squealing pig charged back around the corner of the
house and ran over Longarm. The children followed, knocking the revolver from Longarm's hand and kicking it away.

The elder was frantically reloading his shotgun. From
the house came a chorus of outraged cries. The door slammed
open and the elder's six remaining wives poured out onto
the porch.

"Put down that shotgun!" one of them cried.

"Murderer!" screamed another one.

"You'll kill our children!"

The first one had a cast-iron frying pan. She caught the elder on the top of the head with a blow that made the pan ring. Booth's knees sagged, but he managed somehow to keep upright. The rest of the women, armed with rolling pins, brooms, and in one case a stove poker, fell upon the white-haired elder with a terrible, calculated fury.

Turning to face them, the elder tried to use his shotgun to ward off the blows raining upon him. But the women's outrage, pent up for so long, was no match for Booth. They kicked and they bit, or stood back to measure each blow carefully, until Booth was beaten to his knees as these six Celestial Wives he had taken with him into exile punished him with a brutal, calculating viciousness.

Slowly Longarm got to his feet, mesmerized by the horror of what he was observing. A fierce squeal behind him caused him to duck his head as first the pig, then the shrill band of children swept over him. As soon as they were gone, Longarm scrambled to his feet and raced up the porch steps. Wresting the shotgun from the dazed elder's grasp, he broke it against the porch post, then tried to pull the women off the elder. At once all six turned on him with a fury so terrible it caused him to back away hastily, warding off their blows with upraised forearms. They kept after him like a hive of disturbed bees. Once he was off the porch, the women scrambled back to the elder, catching him as he attempted to crawl back into the house to escape their fury.

Snatching up his sixgun where it had fallen, Longarm watched a scene so incredible he found it difficult to believe. Up on the porch the elder, no longer conscious, was being kicked and assaulted with a relentless, dedicated fury that seemed to have driven the women mad. The elder's immaculate white beard was red with blood. As Longarm watched, a grim, determined effort was being made by two

174

of the women to rip the beard from the elder's face. Meanwhile, with a furious single-minded fury, the others continued to beat at the unconscious man's body with broom handles and rolling pins.

If the elder was not a dead man now, he soon would be. By this time, some of the women were so exhausted by their rage that they were forced to lean back against the porch railing every now and then to catch their breath. Holstering his gun, Longarm turned and beat a hasty retreat.

As he mounted up in front of the mansion, the pack of screeching children swarmed up onto the mansion's front porch after the pig, cornering it in the doorway. Judging from the sudden escalation of squeals that came from the terrified pig, Longarm suspected they might at that moment be throttling the animal with their bare hands.

He turned back around in his saddle and clapped spurs to his mount.

He had seen enough.

Wearing a bottle-green dress with a plunging neckline, Josie Montana glided down the thickly carpeted stairs, her eyes on Longarm, a smile on her face. She was in her late forties, and plump, with clear eyes and teeth that sparkled like pearls above her ruby lips. It was easy to understand why her parlor house did not need to advertise. For a place this deep in the rough mining region, close by the Rubies, she represented a quality these clod-hopping miners rarely approached.

"You asked to see Molly Smith?" she asked, holding out her hand to Longarm.

"Yes, but it's Kristen I want," he told her, brushing the back of her hand gallantly with his lips.

Josie laughed, delighted at the gesture. "She is a friend of yours, Mr. Long?"

He shrugged. "An old . . . acquaintance."

175

"You do not say friend," Josie noted, escorting Longarm to a small living room.

Longarm sat down in an easy chair redolent with perfume. Josie made herself comfortable in a large upholstered armchair across from him. As soon as they were comfortable, the same squat Goshute woman who had let Longarm in placed a bottle of rye whiskey and a shotglass on the ebony tea table before him. For Josie, the woman left a silver tray with a pot of fresh tea and hot muffins. The ladies of the night were still upstairs; Longarm could hear the tinkle of their laughter just above him and could smell the delicious aroma of bacon and eggs as their breakfast was being prepared in the kitchen. It was four o'clock in the afternoon.

"No, I did not say friend," Longarm acknowledged. "But perhaps that was unkind of me."

"Kristen has told me all about it. She was frightened. That was why she unlocked that door. Why don't you forgive her?"

"I guess I already have."

Josie smiled happily. "Good! Kristen needs your help desperately and has been hoping you would return."

"That's why I'm here—to tell her she doesn't have to worry about Elder Booth any longer."

Josie was in the act of pouring herself a cup of tea. She looked up, startled. "Why, whatever do you mean?"

"I mean Booth will no longer be seeking or needing female companionship."

Josie put the pot down. "Would you please be more specific?"

"It is not easy. And you haven't had your breakfast yet."

"Oh, I've long since eaten. It's the girls who'll be fed now. By all means, Mr. Long, go ahead. I have the stomach for any news."

"Elder Booth is dead."

She sat back. "You killed him?"

"No."

"Then who did it?"

"When I saw him last, he was being beaten to death by his wives—all six of them."

"You don't mean that!"

Longarm described to Josie what he had witnessed at the mansion outside of town. Concluding, he suggested this was the last of Elder Booth and his Destroying Angels.

"Are you going to report to the authorities what these women have done to the elder?"

"No, I am not."

"But if what you say is true..."

"If what I say is true, it means that a cruel but effective form of justice has been worked on Elder Booth. For my part, I want no more dealings with those women—or their offspring."

"Yes," Josie said, nodding. She took up her tea and sipped it. "I see your point."

A silence fell over them. Longarm waited for a moment or two for Josie to break the silence, then poured his second drink and leaned back in his chair. He took out a cheroot and lit it, studying Josie closely. "You're stalling, ma'am," he told her finally. "Why?"

"Stalling? Why, whatever do you mean?"

"I came here to see Kristen. You know I want to see her. Yet you keep me down here with a fresh bottle of Maryland rye and send no one up to get her."

"Why, she's sleeping."

"I can hear the girls upstairs. They're having a pillow fight or something—but whatever it is, they ain't sleeping. What're you and Kristen up to?"

Josie feigned surprise, then outrage, but neither worked—especially when she caught the iron glint in Longarm's eyes. She shrugged hopelessly and sighed. "You are right, Mr. Long. Kristen should have known she could not fool someone as observant as you."

"Kristen's gone? She's no longer here?"

"A friend—an old friend, I gather—is upstairs now visiting with her. He came not long before you did. Sometimes I let my girls visit in my upstairs parlor, the place I save for special guests. I am so sorry, Mr. Long. You bring Kristen such good news, I wish you could tell her in person."

Longarm stood up and put on his hat. "Hell, that's not bothering me none, Josie. Kristen and I ain't married, and she's got her own life to live, the way I look at it. And, from what I've seen of her, she'll do fine—just fine."

"She is a *very* lovely girl."

"And tough," he reminded her. "As tough as sawgrass."

"Yes," Josie admitted, getting to her feet. "Allow me to show you out."

"You'll tell her what I told you? That she can forget about the elder now?"

"Yes, I'll tell her," Josie said, as she moved ahead of him through the draped archway that led to the front hall. "And I'm sure she'll be very pleased."

Longarm was moving down the hall to the door when a man's voice behind him commanded: "Hold it right there, Long!"

The voice was heavy, angry—and came from above Longarm. Turning, he saw Pete Walsh on the second-floor landing, a gun in his hand, his left arm wrapped around a terrified Kristen. From the look of her, he had not been treating her well. Using her as a shield, he started down the stairs toward Longarm.

Behind him, Longarm could hear Josie's sharp intake of breath.

"Don't you start screaming, Josie," Pete Walsh warned. "From this distance the only way to stop that would be with a bullet."

Josie did not scream. Behind the gambler on the landing appeared Josie's girls, peering down at them with wide, terrified eyes. Cocking his revolver, Pete smiled coldly at Longarm and continued on down the stairs.

Abruptly, Kristen tried to break free. With a mean chuckle, Walsh squeezed her tighter. Kristen yelped in sudden pain. It sounded to Longarm as if Walsh might have broken a few of her ribs.

Longarm started toward Pete.

"Hold it right there, Long," the gambler told him. "Unbuckle that cross-draw rig of yours, and let it fall to the floor."

By this time Walsh was at the bottom of the stairs, his back to the stairwell. Longarm unbuckled his rig and let it fall.

"Now step away from it," the gambler said, his tight, cold face grim with resolve.

Longarm hesitated.

"Do it or I'll shoot one of them cute little whores up there behind me."

Longarm stepped away from his gun.

Walsh smiled. "I heard you was lookin' for Kristen. A good friend of mine told me. Sam Feeley. So I just been playin' with my old girl friend here, waitin' for you to come visit. Much obliged."

Without warning, Walsh flung Kristen at Longarm. He caught her as she slammed into him and felt her gasp in sudden pain when her ribs slammed into his chest.

"I want to see if I can get two with one shot," Walsh said, grinning. He looked as clean and bright as a new pencil, with unspotted dark coat and pants, white shirt, and black string tie. It was impossible for Longarm to believe that this dandy was Ham Walsh's brother.

Well, he was sure as hell insane enough.

"Move out of the way, Josie," Pete Walsh told her.

Longarm felt Kristen's hand snaking into his vest pocket, the one carrying his derringer. Before he could stop her, she whirled on Walsh. The man stared in sudden shock at the two-barreled weapon in her hand. His delay was fatal. Kristen fired, cocked, and fired again, knocking Walsh back

179

against the banister. But both shots were low, the heavy railroad watch, still depending on its gold-washed chain, pulling her aim down. From two holes in Pete Walsh's stomach came a dark, surging flow that ruined his immaculate pants. The girls watching from the second floor began to scream.

Walsh was still alive. As he slid down the post to the floor, he shot Kristen—then dropped his weapon and died.

Ignoring him, Josie and Longarm rushed to Kristen's side as she crumpled softly to the carpeted floor. Walsh's bullet had caught her in the chest, fatally close to the heart. Already she was having trouble focusing her eyes. Reaching up, she took Longarm's hand.

"This here ain't your fault, Longarm," she told him. "Walsh was the bastard sold me to the elder. He was the gambler I told you about."

"Why did he beat you?"

"He said after he killed you he was going to sell me to Booth a second time. But I told him he'd have to kill me first. That's why he beat me."

Longarm brushed a strand of long, silken hair back off her face.

"He won't beat me no more," she said, "unless I meet him in hell."

Stretching out slightly, she closed her eyes, her head sagging. Quickly, Josie leaned her ear against Kristen's chest, hoping for a heartbeat. With stark eyes she looked back up at Longarm and shook her head.

Longarm got to his feet and looked down at Kristen, then over at the man she had shot to death. Maybe they *would* meet in hell. But if they did, Kristen would be the one with the whip.

He was sure of it. Even the devil has favorites.

On the fifth day after his agreement with Dalton Cross, Longarm topped a rise a few miles from the Lazy S and saw two solid pillars of black smoke pumping into the sky about six miles southwest of his present position—about where he figured Cross's ranch buildings were situated. He smiled. Cross was pulling out, just as he had agreed he would.

A half hour or so later, Longarm reined up and gazed down at the new Lazy S. What he saw pleased him. The ranch house was almost completely rebuilt now, and so were the barns. The blacksmith shop appeared a mite larger than the original and, looking closer at the house, Longarm saw where an addition had been added on to make room for another bedroom or storeroom. The bunkhouse was larger as well. Most of the Mormons were working on the roof of the largest barn, and the sound of their saws and the steady rap of their hammers echoed across the flat.

He could see Sally hanging up clothes on the clothesline beside the house and Harry Wilcox chopping wood alongside the woodshed. From this distance they looked like a man and woman who belonged together. One thing was for sure, Harry was not swinging that axe like a sick man would—and for that he could thank Sally.

Reaching into his inside coat pocket, Longarm took out the letter Sally had sent him, tore it into pieces, and let the wind have it. Then he took out his Colt, lifted it into the air, and fired twice. As the shots echoed across the flat, he saw the work on the ranch come to a halt as each Mormon worker put down his tools and turned in his direction. Sally stepped away from the clothesline. Harry Wilcox put down his axe. They both shaded their eyes as they peered across the flat at him. Then Abe appeared in front of the bunkhouse. Longarm took off his hat and waved. They waved back. Longarm almost thought he could hear Sally calling his name. Clapping his hat back on, he turned his horse about and headed north for Wells.

His vacation, such as it was, had come to an end, and he was almost looking forward to Denver and Billy Vail.

Watch for

LONGARM AND THE GREAT CATTLE KILL

ninety-first novel in the bold
LONGARM series from Jove

coming in July!